Bitter Herbs and Honey

by Barbara Cohen

Lothrop, Lee & Shepard Company
A Division of William Morrow & Company, Inc. • New York

Also by Barbara Cohen

THE CARP IN THE BATHTUB
THANK YOU, JACKIE ROBINSON
WHERE'S FLORRIE?

FOR Leah, Sara, AND Rebecca

1 2 3 4 5 6 7 8 9 10
Library of Congress Cataloging in Publication Data
Cohen, Barbara. Bitter herbs and honey.
SUMMARY: During the early 1900's a young Jewish girl's loyalty to family tradition conflicts with her desire to go to college.
[1. Jews—Fiction. 2. United States—Social life and customs—1865–1918—Fiction] I. Title.
PZ7.C6595Bi 76–18132 ISBN 0–688–41772–8 ISBN 0–688–51772–2 lib. bdg.

Yom Kippur

TWICE A WEEK, on my way home from school, I had to meet the trolley at the corner of Main and Queen streets. In the front of the car, wrapped in brown paper, there would be a package with our name written on it in black crayon. The package contained kosher meat. I would take it off the trolley and carry it home on top of my pile of books.

Carrying Mama's meat home one particular clear, blue, brilliant September afternoon, I happened to say hello to four different people I knew in the half block between the trolley stop and Papa's dry goods store. You couldn't disappear in Winter Hill. I had come there when I was two and it was the only home I could remember. Sometimes its close-knit familiarity seemed to be dragging me down so that I couldn't move. Other times, I felt Winter Hill to be my roots and my support, without which I would float away and never be seen again. It was the beginning of my senior year in high school, and I must admit I was confused a lot of the time.

The last person I met was coming out of my father's store carrying a package. It was Annie Klein. "Oh, Becky," she cried when she saw me, "I just bought such pretty material. The most delicious crepe de chine. It cost a fortune. Sidney'll kill me, but I don't care. Come over and help me lay it out."

"I'll come," I said, "if my mother doesn't need me."

"Good," Annie said. "Stay for supper."

"I can't," I replied. "I've scads of homework."

"Oh, homework." Annie dismissed it airily. "People with marks like yours don't have to do homework."

"How do you think people get marks like mine?" I asked, shaking my head at her frivolity. "Not by not doing their homework!"

"I never did mine," she said, laughing, "and I ended up all right."

"Ended up?" I said. "My goodness, Annie, you're only nineteen, you've barely begun."

"I mean I got as good a husband as any of them."

"Better maybe," I said. "The one thing has nothing to do with the other. Actually, Papa says brains can be a hindrance. Papa says men don't marry girls who show off their intelligence."

"You'd better change your ways then, smarty pants," Annie teased. "I met your chemistry teacher yesterday in Cartland's Pharmacy and we got to talking." He was originally from Newark, like Annie. Besides, Annie "got to talking" with everyone. "He said you were the smartest senior at Winter Hill High, and that's counting all the boys, too, even Peter van Ruysdaal. Keep that up, and you'll never get married!"

"So what?" I said bravely. "Maybe I don't want to get married!"

"Then what would you do?" Annie asked with a laugh. "What else is there?"

"I'll think of something," I said, "but later. If I don't get upstairs now with this stuff, my arms'll fall off."

"See you in a few minutes," Annie called as she went off down the street. I ran around the alley to the back of the store and climbed up to our apartment by the outside stairway. There was an inside stairway, too, in the storeroom behind the shop, but I didn't want to walk through and perhaps drip something on a bolt of cloth from my package of meat which had started to leak.

The fact that there was no kosher butcher in Winter Hill was the bane of my mother's existence. She had to get her meat on the trolley car from New Brunswick. She could not simply walk into a butcher store each day and pick out what she wanted for dinner. She had to leave a standing order with the butcher in New Brunswick and take what he sent her. Most times she didn't like it, and after unwrapping the package I'd brought home, she'd run downstairs to the store and call the butcher on the telephone to tell him that his meat wasn't fit for a dog. But we ate it anyway. It always tasted good to me.

Chickens she could get locally. After fifteen years of living in Winter Hill, New Jersey, it still seemed to her to be located on the very edge of the frontier. But, thank God, she said, for the last seven years since the rabbi had come, she had been able to get a kosher chicken in town. The rabbi was also a *shochet*, a ritual slaughterer. In addition to rabbying, he carried on a thriving chicken business. "What kind of a rabbi is also a butcher?" my mother asked with disdain every Friday morning before she went to his yard to choose a chicken for our Friday night dinner. But she was glad of the opportunity at last to make her poultry selections personally. That made up a little for the rest of the meat.

Mama always said that God had assigned each of us a

task in life. She frequently quoted the Ethics of the Fathers: "It is not required that you complete the task, but neither are you free to abstain from it altogether." If it was her job to live a Jewish life in Winter Hill, she found it a difficult one. And if it was my job to carry home leaky packages of meat, I wasn't so crazy about that either.

"Do you need me, Mama?" I yelled as I tumbled my books and the meat onto the kitchen table.

Mama walked into the kitchen as she heard me. "Don't shout, Rifka," she said. "I'm right here."

"I want to go over to Annie's," I said, lowering my tone obediently. "She just bought a piece of crepe de chine and she wants me to help her lay it out."

"Another piece of material to put on her back?" Mama said, shaking her head disapprovingly. "That girl will drive poor Sidney into the poorhouse." Mama had been hoping Sid would marry Sadie Gratz, a local girl, and though she was no more impervious to Annie's charm than anyone else when she was with her, she did not really trust anyone as pretty and gay as Annie to be a suitable wife to a rising merchant somewhat past his first youth.

"Oh, come on, Mama," I said. "If Sid didn't give her the money, she couldn't spend it, and if he didn't have it, he wouldn't give it to her."

"It'll be different when they have children," my mother predicted darkly. "Let's see how she manages then. She's just a silly child herself!"

"I'm sure she'll rise to the occasion, Mama. You tell

me everybody does. You tell me everybody does what they have to do, even if they don't like it."

"Not everybody," Mama said. "Just sensible people."

The conversation was pointless. "Look, Mama," I said, "can I go or do you need me?"

"Not today," Mama said. "I don't need you today. But tomorrow . . ."

"Of course tomorrow," I said. "Tomorrow I won't go back to school after lunch." The next day was Erev Yom Kippur, the day before the holiest day of the year. In the evening, before we went to Kol Nidre services, Mama would serve a huge dinner, not only to us but to all of Papa's relatives as well. Mama always served a big dinner before a holiday, but on Erev Yom Kippur she served an especially monstrous one because we had to fast until the following evening. Mama believed that in order to prepare for the fast we had to eat more than usual. But we never did, because there's a limit to what a person can consume at one sitting. Mama was unable to grasp this fact and each year prepared, if anything, more than she had the year before. "The children are all much bigger this year," she'd say. "Little Moe will eat like a grown-up this year." If I was to get through the next couple of days, I needed to relax a bit with Annie first.

"Put your books in your room," Mama scolded. "Don't leave them here on the kitchen table where I have to make supper." I obeyed her and then ran out of the apartment, calling a hasty good-bye as I shut the door behind me, leaving her unwrapping the meat and muttering to herself. This meat, obviously, was no better than all the rest.

Annie lived above her in-laws in a two-family house on Queen Street. She had fixed it up in the very latest style. The living-room wallpaper was white with delicate pink roses and the dining-room set was golden oak, instead of dark mahogany like all the other dining-room sets in all the other Jewish homes in Winter Hill. I admired her taste.

She was in the dining room when I arrived. She had already laid her material out on the table and placed the pattern on it. She didn't need me to help her; she was a far better seamstress than I would ever be, but she liked to have someone to talk to while she pinned the pattern to the fabric.

"What's it going to be?" I asked.

"A suit," she said. "The prettiest suit you ever saw. Just like the one they showed in the September issue of *Vogue*." She pointed to the magazine lying open on the sideboard. I glanced at the picture. The opening of the fitted jacket was lined with scallops, as was its slightly flared bottom. No less than five tiers of matching frills were displayed from the bottom of the jacket to the middle of the skirt. The suit was accompanied by the tiniest hat anyone had ever thought of, decorated with a dainty, seductive half veil. I'd certainly never seen anything like it in Winter Hill. "My lord, Annie," I said, "that skirt must be six inches above the ankles."

"It's a copy of a French model," Annie replied complacently. "Too bad I didn't see it sooner. I could have worn it to *shul* on Rosh Hashanah." We had celebrated the Jewish New Year the previous week.

"If you'd shown up in a skirt with five rows of scalloped ruffles, they might have thrown you out," I said. "The Theda Bara hat you wore with the feather sticking up two feet in the air upset them enough."

She laughed. "Got to do something to liven up this dead burg. If I didn't, I think I'd go stark raving mad. I wish I'd get pregnant already."

"You could help in the store," I suggested. All the Jewish women in Winter Hill helped in the store if they weren't nursing tiny babies.

"In a hardware store?" Annie said derisively. "What in the name of heaven would I do in a hardware store?"

"Your mother-in-law . . ." I began.

"Forget my mother-in-law," Annie interrupted. "Sometimes I think she's a man in disguise, and not a very good disguise at that. As long as she's there, I'll certainly never step through the door. Living above her is bad enough. Besides, she'd never let me. You know that."

"You ought to set up as a dressmaker," I suggested.

She nodded. "I wouldn't mind. But Sid would take a fit. He'd say it looked like he needed the money. Besides, I only sew when I feel like it. I really wouldn't make a very conscientious dressmaker." She laughed again. "I guess I'm just not a conscientious person."

"Then maybe it's just as well you're not pregnant," I suggested.

"Oh, I'd be different if I had a baby. I know I would."

Suddenly, though, she was as bored by the subject of herself as she was by Winter Hill. "Get me some more of those pins in that drawer over there," she instructed.

I opened the drawer she indicated and pulled out a paper of pins. "Hey, listen, Becky," she said as she took them from me, "would you like me to make you a dress? I'd love to do it. Look at the one in the book there. It's just a couple of pages after my suit."

I turned the pages of the magazine slowly. "There . . . there . . ." she said. "Turn back . . . it's the page before that one."

I turned back incredulously. "This?" I said. "This one for me? Annie, you're crazy." The white ruffled underskirt was revealed by the slit up the middle of the plum satin sleeveless tunic with a two-foot train trimmed in gold brocade. The neck and the back were cut so low that from the waist up there seemed to be virtually nothing to it. "Where would I go in a dress like this? It's for an actress or someone like that. Not for a schoolgirl in Winter Hill."

"Well," Annie said, "you won't be a schoolgirl much longer. You'll graduate in June. Maybe someone will ask you to a party."

"No one's going to ask me to a party," I assured her.

"Aren't there going to be some parties at graduation time? Aren't you excited about graduating?"

"No," I said coolly, "I'm not excited about graduating."

"Well you should be. Not many girls in Winter Hill —not many Jewish girls—graduate from high school. I think it's marvelous!"

"I don't want school to end," I burst out. "I don't want it to ever end!"

"What!" Annie was shocked. "I couldn't wait. I just couldn't wait until Papa said I could quit. But of course I'm not smart like you. I guess it's different if you're smart."

"I like to study," I admitted. "There's no doubt about that."

"I think you're the crazy one," Annie said. Thoughtfully, she regarded the scissors that she was holding in one hand and the material she was fingering with the other. Then she began to cut. "You like memorizing chemical formulas? You like memorizing the dates of battles? I never heard of such a thing."

"Of course I don't like memorizing things," I said. I despaired of making Annie understand. No one understood, really. There were other good students at Winter Hill High School, but it seemed to me they were good students just because they were naturally quick and ambitious. "I like—I like putting things together. I like seeing the way parts suddenly add up to a whole. And I like losing myself in solving some kind of problem. That's what I like the best. Do you understand?"

Annie hardly heard me. She was busy cutting. "Now I *know* you're crazy," she said lightly. The front panel of the skirt was all cut out now. Annie liked to begin big. I grabbed her hand before she could start on the next piece. I really felt as if I had to make her understand.

"You like to sew, don't you?" I said. "First of all, you're good at it. But you also like to see all these bits and pieces come together. When that happens, when it's all done, you feel as if you've accomplished something. You feel proud. And while you're doing it, nothing else seems to matter, except the thing you're making. Isn't that true?"

Annie looked at me in amazement. "Yes, that's true," she said. "That's why I'm willing to do it, even if it's hard work. But how did you know? You hate to sew. You've told me that a thousand times."

"What do you think I've been trying to tell you, Annie? For me putting one of Cicero's letters into good English is the same as making that crepe de chine suit is for you."

Annie nodded slowly. "I think I understand," she said. "And that's why you don't want school to end."

"That's right," I said. "Maybe it would have been better if they had never sent me to school—to high school, anyway. I mean, I have to know how to read, I have to know how to add and subtract to work in the store. But it would have been better for me if I'd never found out about Shakespeare and Sophocles at all. High school hasn't got anything at all to do with life, at least not with my life!"

"Maybe knowing all that stuff will make you a better person," Annie suggested hesitantly. It didn't sound as if she really believed what she was saying.

I shrugged. "Maybe," I said. "But right now it's only making me unhappy."

"You'll meet a nice young man soon and you'll get married. Then you won't be unhappy anymore," Annie said, picking up her scissors again and starting in on a sleeve. "An intelligent one, who wants an educated wife to produce educated children." She giggled.

"That's right, children who can spout Greek and Hebrew as soon as they're born." I snorted. "Let's not be ridiculous, Annie. Who'd marry me? I'll be seventeen in a month, and no boy has shown the slightest interest in me yet. I'm very plain you know."

"Plain!" Annie stopped cutting and turned to me, shaking her head. "If I had your hair and your figure I'd fall down on my knees and thank God every night. You just don't know what to do with yourself, that's all. You just don't know how to put yourself forward. Not that I blame you. It's not worth the effort for Abe Greenbaum and Solly Gershorn. They're younger than you anyhow. But someone interesting may turn up someday. Someone's cousin or uncle may come to visit. How do you think I met Sid? Your parents will take care to arrange something. And when they do you'd better be ready. You'd better let me make that dress for you."

"But I want to study Greek," I said. "That's what I really want. I know some Hebrew. I know some Latin. I want to know a lot more, and I want to know Greek too."

"But *why?*" Annie asked. "What good would it do you to know Greek?"

"No good at all," I shouted. "No good at all. I just want to know it, that's all." Then I added, in a more restrained tone, "I could teach it or something."

"Oh," Annie said derisively, "there's a big demand for Greek teachers in Winter Hill."

"There are other places in the world besides Winter Hill," I answered. "Or I could teach Latin in the high school. Old Mr. Sondergaard won't live forever."

"The day the Winter Hill school board hires a Jewish teacher will be the day in June that snow falls. Besides, you have to go to college to be a high school teacher. Normal school isn't good enough."

I nodded my head dumbly. I could think of nothing more to say, but I was saved from a further defense of what Annie rightly regarded as my insane notions by the sound of Sid's footsteps on the stairs.

"I'm home," Sid called. "I'm starved. Supper ready?"

"Oh my goodness," Annie whispered, "I'd no idea it was so late. Put this stuff in the drawer, will you? Soon, dear," she called back as she rushed off to the kitchen. "It'll be ready soon."

I began to roll up the material with the pattern pinned to it. Sid came into the dining room. He had to in order to reach the kitchen. "Oh, hello, Becky," he said. "How're you? Been keeping Annie company?" He was a very large man, and his sandy hair was beginning to recede. He looked older than twenty-eight and yet there was a kind of bumbling, youthful quality to him that was somehow endearing. He was like a big, lovable Teddy bear. I wondered why Annie had rushed off to the kitchen so hastily. I had always supposed he let her do whatever she wanted.

"Yes," I said, "I've been keeping Annie company. I've been helping her sew."

He looked down at the material I had gathered into

my arms. "Something new?" he asked. I had no idea of the correct reply so I said nothing. "Staying for dinner?" he added hospitably.

"No," I said, "I've lots of work to do. I have to go."

"Another night, then," he said. "See you in *shul* tomorrow." I nodded and he walked on into the kitchen. I opened the drawer to put away the material. I could not help hearing his conversation with Annie.

"Hello, darling," he said. I heard her footsteps as she ran to him. For a moment there was silence and then he said, "I'm starved. I could eat a horse."

"Dinner will be ready soon," she said.

There was a pause again, briefer this time, and then I heard him say, "But you haven't even begun, have you? Not really."

"Oh, Sidney," she said, "I'm so sorry, really I am, but the time just went by. Please forgive me."

"We can go down and eat with Mama," Sidney said. "She asked us to come in, but I said I was sure you'd have dinner ready. After what we talked about yesterday, I was sure you'd have dinner ready."

"But I will," Annie said. "I will in a minute. Let's not go downstairs. It'll be ready in a minute."

"No it won't," Sidney said. "It won't be ready for an hour, and I'm hungry." His voice held a note of annoyance that I had never heard before and I suddenly realized I should not be listening. I closed the drawer with the material in it.

"Good night, Annie," I called. "Good night, Sidney. See you tomorrow." Before either of them could make an attempt to see me out, I rushed through the parlor and down the steps.

The next day in school Mr. Allison, who taught us chemistry and trigonometry, made an announcement. Mr. Allison was new that year. He was very young and had lots of ideas. He said that he had decided the Winter Hill High School senior class should issue an annual. He said that the high school he had graduated from, in Newark, had had an annual. He showed it to us. It was a book of studio portraits of each member of the graduating class with a brief biography underneath. It had other pictures, too, of things like the debating society and the football team and the Latin club. Beneath their photographs, his friends had written little messages and signed their names. "Lots of luck to West Side's science genius. Your friend, Gladys Royal." "I'll never forget the good times in Miss Hutt's English class. Minnie." "All the best, old pal. Bill." In eighth grade we had had autograph books. As a remembrance, an annual was obviously several cuts above that level and much more suitable to our increased age and dignity. We agreed that Winter Hill High really needed one now that it had grown to be a school of nearly three hundred students, with a graduating class of forty-two. Mr. Allison had done the preliminary work. He had been in touch with Mr. Dale at the Photographic Studio and Mr. Stoneman, who printed *The Republican Gazette*. Both had said they'd be glad to work with us.

"And now, I think I'll appoint a committee to get this thing started," Mr. Allison said. He glanced around the room. "Peter," he said. That went without saying. Peter was the leader in everything. "Dick Evans. Mabel, and let's see, one more girl—Rebecca. That's Peter van Ruysdaal, Dick Evans, Mabel Mortimer, and Rebecca Levitsky. You four stay for a moment after class and see if you can agree on a meeting time."

Chemistry was our last class before lunch, so we gathered at Mr. Allison's desk after the others had left. "We could stay after school tomorrow," Peter said, "and get started. I have football practice, but I can tell the fellows I'll be a few minutes late and, after I leave, Dick can handle things." Dick was Peter's sidekick, always taking over where Peter left off.

"I can't come after school tomorrow," I said. "I won't be coming back after lunch."

"Why not?" Mr. Allison asked. "Planning to come down with the grippe right after lunch?" Sometimes I didn't like Mr. Allison.

"Don't be silly, Mr. Allison," Mabel said. "Rebecca never misses school unless she has to. It must be another one of her holidays. Remember, she was out two days last week?"

"That's right, Mr. Allison," I said. "It's the eve of the Day of Atonement. We have to fast and pray for twenty-four hours."

Mr. Allison nodded. "Oh, I know all about Yom Kippur," he said. "I knew lots of Jews in high school and college. But just this once, couldn't you . . ."

"Have the meeting without me," I interrupted. "I'll come to the next one."

"We need you," Peter said.

"If they can manage without you, after you go to practice, they can certainly manage without me," I said with a smile.

"We need you a lot more than we need me," Peter said. "You're the writer."

"Well," said Mr. Allison, "that'll come later. It *is* important to get started. A book like this takes a lot of time to get together."

"I don't want to meet without Becky," Peter said firmly. "Suppose she was calling a meeting, and she decided to have it on Christmas day and we couldn't come. Would that be right? Two days aren't going to make any difference."

I looked at Peter in amazement. Though he had been a year ahead of me until I skipped fifth grade, I had known who he was since first grade. I knew his father, who owned the biggest lumberyard in central New Jersey. I knew his mother, who was a customer in my father's store. The van Ruysdaals were an important family in Winter Hill, where their ancestors had settled long before the American Revolution. But obviously I did not know Peter van Ruysdaal very well, because I would never have imagined his saying what he had just said!

"Peter's right," Dick echoed. "We'll have the meeting Monday after school."

"Is that O.K., Becky?" Peter asked, turning to me.

"Oh, yes, that's fine," I said. I was a little flustered. I was not accustomed to being deferred to by my classmates. I thought about it all the way home. I had always known Peter to be a fine athlete, an excellent student and a leader of men—sort of the Teddy Roosevelt of Winter Hill High School. But I had never thought of him as sensitive and understanding. We had barely a nodding acquaintance, so his concern was not the result of friendship.

I ate lunch with Mabel Mortimer on winter days when we brought brown paper bags instead of walking home. She'd be more likely to consider my feelings out of friendship, and yet it hadn't occurred to her to do so. Only to Peter.

I helped my mother all that afternoon. So did Ruth. We had a lot to do because this was dinner:

Chopped chicken livers

Gefilte fish

Chicken soup with *matzoh* balls

Challah

Roast chicken

Noodle pudding

A *tzimmes* of carrots and apples

Celery, olives, and pickles

Pot roast of beef

Applesauce

Sponge cake

Taiglach

Sliced peaches

Tea

Besides Mama, Papa, Ruth, and me, these are the people who sat down with us for dinner: Uncle Moishe, Aunt Rachel, Henry Braude, Aunt Branna, Cousin Benny, Cousin Zelda, Cousin Claude, Uncle Simon, Aunt Gittel, Cousin Fanny, Cousin David, Little Moe, Baby Maude, Aunt Dorothy, Uncle Daniel, Cousin Albert, Cousin Milly and Cousin Leo.

The parlor wasn't big enough to hold all of us and we had no dining room. The younger children had to sit in the kitchen. That meant Ruth, Fanny, Milly, Leo, Little Moe, and Baby Maude, who was sitting up at the table for the first time that year. My cousin Albert and I were, for the first time, promoted to the main table in the parlor. There was no surer sign of impending adulthood. But it surprised me a little when Mama told me.

"I'm a year younger than Albert," I said, "and this is the first year you've let him sit in the parlor."

"You sit next to Henry Braude and be nice to him," Mama said. "He's a stranger, and he must be lonesome."

"Why can't Uncle Moishe and Aunt Rachel sit next to Henry Braude and be nice to him?" I said. "They live in the same house. They know him; I don't."

"Maybe Henry Braude is tired of your Aunt Rachel and Uncle Moishe," Mama said. "Maybe he'd like a nice pleasant young woman to talk to for a change. What kind of house is Moishe's for a young man? It's about as lively as a funeral parlor. All any of them in that house think about is work, work, work, money, money, money." My mother would cook and scrub for weeks in advance when she knew my father's family was coming, and complain about them the whole time. Especially about his oldest brother, Moishe, and Moishe's wife, Rachel. Much of my father's family lived in Winter Hill, like us, or in the neighboring town of Brookville. Mama's family, what there was of it, was on New York City's East Side and we didn't see them nearly as often.

I dutifully sat next to Henry Braude, as I had been instructed. This was the first I had met him, though of course I had heard that he was a distant cousin of Aunt Rachel's and had come to help Uncle Moishe in the store. Papa said it was a marvelous opportunity for a young man because Uncle Moishe and Aunt Rachel were childless, but Mama said they wouldn't give away coals in the summertime and, besides, they'd probably outlive the poor fellow, having worked him to death.

But I decided that Henry Braude had been made to order for Uncle Moishe and Aunt Rachel. "It must be hard," I said politely, "leaving your family behind and moving out here to the country."

"I miss Mama and Papa, of course," he said with the careful precision of a man who's only recently learned English but is determined not to let that fact show, "but I don't miss New York. I didn't live there so long anyway." He could not erase every trace of a Yiddish accent, but his English was excellent for someone who had been in the United States only three years, and I told him so. He smiled a little and his brown eyes peered at me from behind his thick lenses. "I studied hard. I understand you too are a student," he said.

I nodded. Someone had been telling him about me, which I found very curious. "I like languages especially," I said.

"Not very useful in this country," he said. "In this country newcomers must learn English fast if they want to get ahead. No other language is necessary. I'm really grateful to your aunt and uncle for this opportunity. The store does very well, and I am sure I can help it to do much, much better."

"I'm sure," I agreed. His self-confidence and his cavalier dismissal of anything not immediately practical would certainly endear him to Uncle Moishe, but they weren't likely to endear him to me.

"You should devote your excellent mind," he instructed me, "to studies you can make use of. You should be studying bookkeeping and perhaps typewriting. Things useful in a business like your father's—or your uncle's."

There were times when I had thought so myself, but I didn't like someone else saying so.

He was really beginning to annoy me. "How do you know my mind is excellent?" I said.

He smiled his thin smile again. "Ah-ha," he said, "I have my informants."

Suddenly, in the back of my mind, I could hear Annie Klein's voice. "Your parents will take care to arrange something," she had said to me only the day before. "Your parents will take care to arrange something."

Henry Braude was still talking. "A good mind is a valuable asset in the retail business. But if you're going to work in a store, you must make practical use of it. You want to be helpful to your father in his store, don't you? Or to your husband, if he should happen to be a retail merchant?"

I felt hot with embarrassment, and to cover it I said in a loud, clear voice, "I hope your mysterious informants knew what they were talking about. I have no intention of working in my father's store when I graduate from high school."

Henry was not the only one who heard me. My Uncle Simon, the husband of my father's sister Gittel, was sitting opposite me. He heard me too. He was a huge man with black hair and a black beard and a deep black voice to match. My remark startled him enough to make him lower the chicken leg he was lifting to his mouth at that very moment. Anything that deflected Uncle Simon from the major activity of his life—eating—really had to be remarkable. "What do you mean, Becky?" he said. "What do you mean, you're not going to help your father? This is the first I hear of it." He turned toward my father at the head of the table. "What's going on here, Chaim?" he bellowed. "No one ever told me Becky wasn't going to work in the store. What is she going to do?"

My father just smiled. "Oh, she'll work in the store, Simon," he said. "Don't be foolish. She's just talking. She doesn't want school to be over. You know our Becky!" My father was very calm. He never let even his own brothers and sisters see how he really felt. This was the first time he'd heard me mention my reluctance to embark on the path marked out for all nice Jewish girls—helping in their fathers' stores until they married. However, he acted as if we'd talked about it dozens of times, only shooting me a quizzical glance out of his sharp blue eyes. I knew that he'd have a lot to say in private.

"Doesn't want school to be over?" Henry said. "What does she want to do? Go to college?" His tone was heavy with derision.

College had never occurred to me. Jewish girls didn't go to college. Only rich Gentiles and poor orphans, like in *Daddy Long Legs*, which was Ruthie's favorite book that year. "I never thought about going to college," I said.

"Of course not," Henry said approvingly. "College is foolishness. It's for wealthy *goyim*."

Henry's agreement turned out to be worse than his disagreement. "Doctors and lawyers?" I asked sardonically. "Are they a lot of foolishness?"

"Oh, well," Henry dismissed me, "if a man wants a career in a profession instead of business, that's different. Of course he has to go to college. Naturally I believe in education."

"Oh, naturally," I said.

He looked at me. "But there is absolutely no need for a woman to go to college," he said. "There isn't even any need for a woman to go to high school."

"Oh, you're right." I smiled sweetly. "Why, they shouldn't even bother to teach us to read and write."

It finally dawned on him that I was baiting him. "You're teasing me, Miss Rebecca," he said. "I think it's very nice you go to high school. It gives you accomplishments. It's nice for a woman to have accomplishments. But they aren't necessary." His tone struck me as unbearably condescending.

I was about to make another one of what my mother called my smart answers when, in Yiddish, she told me to clear the table. Henry Braude, and every other person at the table over twenty-one, understood Yiddish better than I did, but my mother always spoke Yiddish when she was under the influence of a strong emotion. She was annoyed with me. There was no doubt about it.

Fortunately, I was so busy for the rest of the meal that I had little opportunity to speak to Henry Braude or anyone else. Services began at six. We had sat down for dinner at four-thirty, so it was something of a rush to get all those courses in. The men left as soon as they had finished eating; the women stayed for a little while to help Mama clean up, but she soon shooed them off. She really couldn't stand so many underfoot in her kitchen. "Go to *shul*," she said. "God is waiting for you."

"Not without you, Molly," my Aunt Branna said to her. "We'll all clean up, it'll go faster."

"I'll help Mama," I said. "The rest of you go. The kitchen can't hold so many."

"You go too, Rifka," Mama insisted. "Just leave me alone to get it done in my own way."

"Mama, I'll stay, I'll help," I said. I stood next to her and spoke softly. "I want to stay. I want to help you. I don't care if I get to *shul* late. Who needs to get there so early to sit in the back?"

"Rebecca," Mama said firmly, though in a voice as low as mine, "you go. You go right this minute. I have had enough nonsense from you tonight. I don't need anymore."

"What are you talking about? What did I do?"

"We'll discuss it later. Not now. Just get out! God is most especially waiting for you!"

I could not think of anything to say that would not make her angrier, so I left with my aunts. Because they did not want to miss Kol Nidre, we rushed down the street to the large room above Jones's Milling which the Jews of Winter Hill rented from Mr. Jones for all their communal activities, including religious services. A room above a feed and grain store is not the ideal location for such activities. It is inclined to attract unwelcome visitors like rats and mice, no matter how frequently it is swept out. But it was the only place available to us where thirty-five families, from Brookville as well as Winter Hill, amounting to something like a hundred and fifty people, could collect at one time.

As a matter of fact, at a time like Yom Kippur, when every one of us actually was present, Allemand Hall, as it was called, was really too small. By dint of much persuasion, not all of it gentle, my father and others like him had finally gathered together enough money to buy a piece of property at the east end of Main Street from old Mrs. Dougherty for a synagogue. The ground had been broken ceremoniously, and the cornerstone laid. It was our hope that by next Rosh Hashanah we would be worshipping there. But this year, for the last time, we would have to make do with Allemand Hall.

My aunts and I had to squeeze to find seats in the back of the room behind the screen where the women sat. Literally every Jew from our end of the county was present, except for the handful of women like my mother who were still washing up. Even they would be along soon.

The Baumgartners and the Goldbergs and the Bauers were present too. They were the Germans, the old Jews who had been in town for thirty or forty years. Until we had come, they had held a *minyan* in Mr. Bauer's house and they did not like the rest of us, because at best, we were Russian greenhorns, and at worst, ignorant, pushy, and common. For a long time they had continued to hold their weekly *minyan* in Mr. Bauer's house rather than join us at Allemand Hall.

Mr. Baumgartner had been the first to recognize the folly of this path, and with my father and some other Russians he had formed a *chevra kadisha*, a burial society, which a handful of German Jews could not have managed by themselves. The *chevra kadisha* had been the nucleus of the group that had eventually managed to break ground for the synagogue, a thing most of Mr. Baumgartner's friends had not been able to resist. There were one or two holdouts among the Germans but they were those who hardly counted as Jews anyway.

This was the first year the Baumgartners, the Goldbergs, the Bauers and the other German families had joined us for Rosh Hashanah and Yom Kippur. I supposed they had come this year so that next year, when the synagogue was ready, they wouldn't shock the rest of us by showing up all of a sudden.

I eyed Mrs. Goldberg and Mrs. Baumgartner and their three daughters all lined up in the first row of the women's section. Though this was the first year they had come, they had automatically taken the seats of precedence. In their dark but well-tailored silk suits and modest hats they did not look Jewish to me. They looked like the Winter Hill ladies I saw every Sunday walking down Queen Street to the First Reformed Church. I looked with particular interest at Ella Goldberg. She had gone to normal school in Trenton and now taught second grade in New Brunswick, where the school board was a little more liberal in its outlook than the one in Winter Hill. She went there every day on the trolley. I didn't want to teach second grade, though. I wanted to teach Latin or Greek, if I taught at all.

It was a good thing I had the German ladies to watch and think about, because the service was so remote that it meant almost nothing to me. I could read Hebrew because my father had taught it to me. This gave me an advantage over most of the other ladies sitting behind the *mechitza*, the screen that separates men and women in an Orthodox Jewish synagogue. Most of them simply gossiped quietly with each other and tried to keep their children in reasonably good order. They had been silent when I had first come in for the chanting of the Kol Nidre prayer with which the Yom Kippur service opened. Its plaintive melody seems to move even the most tenuous of Jews, and all of us chanted it together twice more after the rabbi had done. After that it was more or less every person for himself, and I lost interest, as usual. For me the least of Judaism was what went on in the synagogue, where men counted for so much more than women.

But the next day, by the time I had fasted for nearly twenty-four hours and had returned to the synagogue for the services that marked the end of the long day of abstinence and prayer, a feeling of elation had overcome me. I was beyond hunger and felt only a kind of pure exhaustion. It was as if my physical self had been put aside for a moment and I really was communicating with God in an effort to atone for and be forgiven my sins. I could feel this even behind the *mechitza*, even at my distance from the service's center. God knew, and I knew, that of the hundred or so sins listed in the confessional we were all reciting there were several that applied directly to me.

For the sin which we have committed before Thee
by spurning parents and teachers,
And for the sin which we have committed before
Thee in presumption or in error,
For the sin which we have committed before Thee
by stretching forth the neck in pride,
And for the sin which we have committed before
Thee by idle gossip,
And for the sin which we have committed before
Thee by contentiousness,
And for the sin which we have committed before
Thee by being stiff-necked,

For all these, O God of forgiveness, forgive us,
pardon us, grant us atonement.

With the final sounding of the *shofar*, the ram's horn,
an almost audible sigh of relief ran though the congregation. I turned to kiss my mother and sister.
"*L'Shanah Tovah*," we said. "A good year." We were
back to normal now, ready for the simple pleasure of
the good cold meal of hard-boiled eggs, rye bread, and
herring which awaited us at home. We'd eat apples too,
dipped in honey to symbolize the sweet year for which
we all had just finished praying.

My mother and sister were beside me as we left
Allemand Hall. But I lost them in the little crowd that
had gathered in front of the building to exchange the
final greetings of the season. I was looking for Annie
Klein, whom I hadn't managed to see all day, when
suddenly Henry Braude appeared at my side. "May I
walk home with you?" he asked.

"Walk home with me?" I was startled. I knew what
that meant, and I didn't like it very much. But after all
there was no possible reason to deny him. I looked
about me hastily, hoping that my mother or father
would appear to accompany us and, indeed, there was
my mother just a few feet from me talking to Mrs.
Gershenson. I beckoned to her and she came toward
me. "Henry's walking home with us," I called. "He
can get the trolley to Brookville at our corner." I
didn't want him hanging around all evening.

"Go ahead without us," Mama said. "We'll be along
in a few minutes. You'll stay and break the fast with us,

Henry. You can get the trolley later." It was not an invitation; it was an order.

We started up the street. My mother had deserted me. She had never done that before. I was too busy fuming over that to bother making conversation with Henry and we walked for a while in silence.

"A penny for your thoughts, Miss Rebecca," Henry said at last with heavy jocularity.

"I wouldn't sell you my thoughts for ten dollars." It hadn't taken me long to get back to the sin of being stiff-necked. But Henry didn't appear to notice. It seemed to me that he thought too well of himself and too infrequently of anyone else to catch an implied insult.

"Then you must be thinking of me," he said. "I hope they are positive thoughts, Miss Rebecca!"

"I have nothing against you, Henry," I said. "After all, we've just met. But we don't seem to share many ideas, do we?"

"Your ideas may change," he said. "I hope you're not—rigid."

" 'A foolish consistency,' " I quoted, " 'is the hobgoblin of little minds.' " We were reading Emerson in Miss Krieter's English class. "But that goes for men as well as women," I added. "I hope *you're* not rigid."

"Goodness, no," Henry hastened to reassure me. "I've got lots of new ideas. There are so many things I could do with Cousin Moishe's store, if only he'd let me. That's really the only source of conflict between us. Not that he knows it. I keep quiet, of course—now. But my opportunity will come."

"And you will know how to make use of it," I said.

"No doubt about it," he replied firmly. "Cousin Moishe doesn't realize that his clientele is changing. It isn't just farmers anymore looking for Levis and work shoes that last forever. The young women in town read the *Ladies' Home Journal*. They want the latest styles, and he should stock them. No one else in Brookville carries really classy ready-to-wear." He began to describe the kind of store Levitsky's of Brookville would be if he had charge of it, and he was so carried away by his visions of plate-glass windows, bright electric lights and ornately decorated gold cash registers that he was still talking when we got home, where, thank goodness, my parents and Ruth caught up with us.

I did not have to say much during supper either. It was obvious that once Henry got started, there was no stopping him. He and my father spent most of the evening discussing small town vs. big city merchandising. That is, mostly Henry discussed and my father listened. After Henry had left, Papa said, "That's a very bright young man. He's got a lot to learn, but he's smart enough to learn it."

"If he keeps quiet long enough to hear what someone else has to say," I commented sharply.

"I don't like your attitude toward him at all," Mama said. We were in the kitchen, washing up. Papa was sitting in his rocker by the stove, half reading the paper, half talking to us. "You should be nice to him," she went on. "He's a stranger."

"I'd like to talk to you about that," I said, all my suspicions gathering themselves together in my mind.

"Why all of a sudden are you so anxious for me to be nice to strangers in town?"

"What do you mean, 'all of a sudden'?" Mama said. "We are always nice to newcomers. There are so few of us, you know we have to stick together."

"When Annie Klein came to town you didn't urge me to be nice to her," I said.

"That's different," Mama said. "She has a husband."

"Henry has cousins," I reminded her.

"For a smart girl," Mama said between her teeth, "you are very thick."

"Molly," Papa interrupted, "be honest with the child. Look here, Rebecca," he said, addressing himself to me as he laid his paper aside, "this is a very small town. Not many eligible Jewish young men come your way and your mother just thinks that . . . well, you should be nice to everyone you meet . . ." He seemed to hesitate for a moment and then he finished up quickly, ". . . and make the most of every opportunity."

"So that's it," I said. "You want me to marry Henry Braude. I suspected something like that!"

"You're jumping to conclusions," Papa said. "Who said anything about marry?"

"What makes you think Henry Braude wants to marry you," my mother said, "after the way you've acted?"

"This is not Russia," I said. "Here the marriages are not arranged." I was really angry.

"Rebecca, I told you," Papa said, "we are not talking about marriage. You are too young for anything like that."

"I was seventeen when I married you, Chaim," Mama reminded him.

"Rebecca's going to finish school," Papa said. "Then she can work in the store a year or so before she has to think of anything like marriage."

"I don't want to work in the store," I blurted out.

"Yes," Papa replied calmly, "I heard you say that before. Yesterday at dinner."

"I assumed," Mama said, "that it was something you said just to annoy Henry."

"I really don't want to work in the store," I repeated. "It's no joke."

"Then what will you do?" my father asked reasonably. "You have to do something until you get married. You've just told us Henry Braude's not an acceptable candidate, and I don't notice anyone else on the horizon."

"Husbands don't grow on trees," my mother said. "They're not so easy to find."

I shook my head. "There must be something I can do," I said. "Something besides work in the store until I get married. Something a smart girl like me can do."

"Smart, smart," Papa said. "What good is smart?"

"Humph," Mama commented, "who taught her to read Hebrew when she was four years old? Who cried when she got the literature prize at the eighth-grade graduation? If you didn't want her to be smart, you should never have gotten her started on it."

"She's like me," Papa said. I began to feel as if I weren't in the room. "If you're interested in things like that," he went on, "you don't need anyone to start you—and no one can stop you. But those things don't do you any good. They aren't any use."

"Now you sound like Henry," I said. "Maybe I could be a teacher."

"You'd have to go away to normal school," Mama said. "What would you eat?"

"Ella Goldberg went to normal school," I said.

"I'm sure the Goldbergs don't care if they eat *treife* or not," Mama said primly. (*Treife* is non-kosher meat.)

"I never knew you wanted to be a teacher," Papa said. "You never mentioned anything about it before."

I didn't want to be a teacher. At least not a teacher in an elementary school such as the normal schools turned out.

"I'd like to learn Greek," I said, "and more Latin and Hebrew too. I'd like to study ancient languages and civilizations."

"But why?" he asked me again.

"I don't know." I shook my head slowly. "It's just what I want to do. The languages and the civilizations both—it's like putting together the pieces of a jigsaw puzzle. I love it. I've been reading about the excavations at Pompeii. I have this book I got from the library. I'll show it to you."

I made a move toward the room I shared with Ruth. Papa stopped me. "That won't be necessary," he said. "I'm sure it's very interesting. I'll look at it later. But right now, you come here, Becky."

I went over to him. "Sit down," he said. I sat on the bright rag rug at his feet, as I had done so often when I was a little girl to listen to him tell me tales of his childhood in the little *shtetl* of Marminsk in Poland. That was the happy part. Then came the sad part when he spoke of the big boat with hundreds of poor Jews crowded into its hold. He had traveled on that boat to come to America all by himself at the age of sixteen. How my heart had ached for that boy who had said a tearful farewell to the tubercular mother he was never to see again as he set out on the lonesome journey to a father he could barely remember and a strange new land whose tongue he could not speak. Perhaps as I sat at his feet once more, Papa was thinking of these old stories too.

"Becky," he said, "you know that we want to do the best for you and Ruth. That's why we're here—in America, in Winter Hill."

I nodded. "Of course I know that, Papa," I said.

"We're very proud of you," he went on. "We think it's wonderful that you read books like this one about Pompeii."

"And *The Decline and Fall of the Roman Empire*," I added. "You'd like that one, Papa. It's all about how Christianity ruined Rome."

"I'll have to look at it," Papa said. Papa liked to read, but he did not read English easily. I wondered if I could get *The Decline and Fall* in a Yiddish translation. "I'm glad you like to read books like that and I hope you go on reading them all your life, but working in the store isn't going to stop you from reading books."

"I wish I could earn my living," I said. "I wish I could earn my living some other way than working in the store."

"Earn your living?" Papa said. "It will not be necessary for you to earn your living. You can help in your husband's store, if he has one."

"And do your housework," Mama said, "and raise your children. That will keep you busy enough."

"That's earning a living," I pointed out, "even if it isn't working for pay, and I'd rather do it in other ways. Maybe I won't get married. That's possible. Look at Sadie Gratz. She must be twenty-five and she's not married." I paused for a moment and looked at the shocked expressions on both their faces. "Maybe I won't want to get married!"

"My God!" Mama threw up her hands in despair. "What did I tell you, Chaim?" she said to Papa. "What did I tell you would happen if we moved to a small town like this one? You can't be a Jew here, that's what I told you."

"We had to make a living, Molly," Papa said. "And we do make a living. We make a good one."

"A living isn't everything," Mama said. "We can't even keep the sabbath out here. You have to work in the store on Saturday, and I have to help you. God is punishing us for that."

"God wouldn't have wanted us to starve," Papa said. "We're doing the best we can."

"A living isn't everything," Mama repeated.

"Without it, there's nothing else," Papa insisted.

"She doesn't want to get married," my mother groaned. "She doesn't want to get married. Whoever heard of a Jewish girl saying such a thing? Whoever heard of any girl saying such a thing?"

I jumped up and ran over to her. I put my arms around her. "You're making too much of this, Mama," I said. "I'm not sure I don't want to get married. I just meant not marrying is a possibility, like with Sadie Gratz, and a person ought to be prepared for it."

"Sadie's prepared," Papa said. "Sadie's a bookkeeper at Hogan's Furniture Store. Do you want to be a book-keeper? You can barely add two and two."

"Look, Papa," I said. "I don't want to be a book-keeper at Hogan's Furniture Store, and I don't want to marry Henry Braude, and I don't even want to go to normal school in Trenton. But I want to do something, and that something is *not* working for you."

"Listen to me," Papa said firmly, "you've got almost a year to make up your mind what that something is. And whatever it is, it'll have to be something proper, something suitable for a daughter of mine to be doing."

"And it'll have to be something that a Jewish girl can do," Mama added, "something that a Jewish girl can do and still be Jewish."

"You have your minds already made up, don't you?" I said angrily. "Proper for *your* daughter," I went on, glancing at Papa, "and Jewish," I added to Mama. "What's that but working in the store and getting married? Well, I won't do either. You wait and see. I'll think of something."

"Keep a civil tongue in your head, young lady," Papa said, getting up out of the chair. He turned to Mama. "I'm going to bed," he told her. "Sitting in *shul* all day without eating is enough to kill me, without a discussion like this on top of it. Rebecca," he said to me, "whatever you do, it will be what your mother and I think is suitable for you to do." With that he turned and walked out of the room.

"You're crazy . . ." my mother began, but I interrupted her.

"I'm tired, too," I said. "I'm going to bed. There's nothing more to say. Not now, anyway."

I didn't usually run from a verbal battle, but I was too exhausted from the long day's fast to fight. Besides, what was the point? Maybe Papa could make me work in the store, but Mama couldn't make me marry Henry Braude if I didn't want to!

Sukkos

OUR APARTMENT HAD a back porch. It was really just the roof of the back part of the store, with a rail around it. It was here each fall that Papa built three sides of our *sukkah*. The fourth side was the kitchen's outside wall. Its roof was just a few branches laid across the top and hung with gourds, Indian corn, and apples. The hut was small, but large enough to hold a small table and a couple of chairs. According to Jewish law we were supposed to take all our meals in the hut during the eight days of the festival of Sukkos, but most nights Papa just made *kiddush* by blessing the festival wine in the booth, and then we went inside for dinner. In New Jersey, unlike Palestine, open-air dining in October is not always reasonable.

I did not stay home from school the first two days and the last two days of the holiday either, any more than Papa kept the store closed those days. In spite of Mama's objections, it was enough for both of us that we had lost time for Rosh Hashanah and Yom Kippur the previous month.

On the second day of Sukkos we had a meeting after school about the annual. We had decided to call it *Parnassus*, which we regarded as the literary equivalent of the football team's nickname, "Mountaineers." We were lucky that day because Peter van Ruysdaal was able to work with us. It had started to rain about one o'clock. An hour later it was really teeming, so football practice had been canceled.

Four other students had joined our original committee and Peter gave each one of us a job. Mabel and

I were to write the captions underneath both the senior portraits and the pictures of the teams and clubs. Actually, when you came down to it, we were to write the whole book. It was going to be quite a job because we would have to approach each senior individually and get him to put down his high school activities, his favorite subjects, his future plans. And we wanted to find appropriate literary quotations to appear beneath each portrait. Things like "A star danced and under that was I born" for Beatrice Collier, who, like her namesake, happened to be a bright, lively girl. They weren't all that easy. We were afraid it would take us six months to find an appropriate quotation for Harold Rackworth, who had barely exchanged two words with any of us in the twelve years we'd known him.

"How about 'Silence is golden'?" Mabel suggested.

"That might hurt his feelings," I said. "What do you think of 'Between true friends there is no need of speech'?"

"Perfect!" Mabel agreed, hastily scribbling it down in her notebook, as Peter joined us. He had been wandering from group to group, getting each one started. He was a born leader because he knew how to delegate authority. At least that's what Mr. Allison said.

"What's perfect?" Peter asked.

" 'Between true friends there is no need of speech,' " Mabel repeated. "Do you think that's good for Harold Rackworth?"

"Use it, use it!" Peter was enthusiastic. "You'll never find a better one. Who said it?"

"Me," I replied. "I just made it up."

Peter looked at me and laughed. "That's the stuff," he said. "I knew you were the right one for this job."

"It'll be fine," Mabel said, "so long as we don't have to put down the source of each quote."

"I can make that up too," I replied calmly. "Ibrahim ben Yosef. How does that sound?"

"Sort of like Abou ben Adhem," Peter said. "Abou ben Adhem" was a poem by Leigh Hunt that we'd all had to memorize in eighth grade.

"Exactly," I agreed.

"Hey, Mr. Allison," Peter called. Mr. Allison was talking to Dick Evans and Gilbert Smith about setting up appointments at the photographer's studio for each of the seniors, but he left them and came over to us. "Listen to this," Peter said. "For Harold Rackworth." He took the sheet of paper from Mabel's desk and read, " 'Between true friends there is no need of speech.' You know that one, don't you?"

"Oh sure," Mr. Allison said. "Very familiar. Perfect for Harold Rackworth. Had it on the tip of my tongue myself!"

I turned away so I could swallow my laughter.

"Do you remember who said it?" Peter asked. I did not know how he could go on without a crack in the sincere, eager expression he wore on his handsome face.

Mr. Allison hesitated a moment and then said, "Uh . . . uh . . . Emerson! Emerson said it, I think."

"That's close," Peter said. "It was Ibrahim ben Yosef."

I was in control of myself now. "Abou ben Adhem's cousin," I added brightly.

"Yes, of course," Mr. Allison said.

"He's often called the Arab Emerson," I said. "No wonder you got them confused."

"Miss Krieter gave me some Emerson essays," Mr. Allison said. Though she was years older than he, it was perfectly clear to all of us that Miss Krieter had a crush on Mr. Allison. Mr. Allison was terribly handsome. He looked just like the man in the Arrow shirt advertisements. "Come up to my desk," he told me, "and get it. Maybe it'll give you some more ideas."

I followed him to his desk. He opened the drawer and took out two books. "I would appreciate it very much," he said almost in a whisper, "if you would do me a little favor. Your friend, Annie Klein—you know she left high school to get married."

I merely nodded. It was a strange remark.

"I run into her now and then in Cartland's Pharmacy. We got to talking. After all, we're both from Newark."

I nodded again. Whatever it was he wanted to say, I didn't intend to make it easy for him.

"She's very interested in furthering her education."

"Oh?" I replied coolly. "I didn't know that."

"I promised I'd help her," he went on quickly. "I promised I'd lend her some books. Will you take these to her, please? Tell her to take her time with them. I don't need them back."

I turned the books he had given me over in my hand so I could see their spines. One was, indeed, Emerson's *Essays*. The other was *Sonnets from the Portuguese* by Elizabeth Barrett Browning. I held it up. "The very thing," I said sweetly, "that Annie needs to fill in the gaps in her education. The very thing."

He looked at me darkly, but I only smiled. "I didn't think she'd want anything too heavy to start with," he said.

"No, of course not," I agreed. "Any message?"

"No, no message. Why would there be a message?"

"I don't know," I said. "Some instructions."

"We'll discuss the poems," he said formally, "next time I see her in Cartland's."

"Good," I said. "I'll tell her that."

Peter appeared at my side. "I think we'd better go now, Mr. Allison," he said. "It's getting late, and we've done all we can for today."

Mr. Allison nodded. "All right," he called to the group, "we'll stop now. Each of you can get together with his own committee when he has a chance, and we'll all meet again next Thursday after school."

"It's pouring," Isabel Liebig said as she rose from her desk. "We're all going to get soaked going home. It was just a little cloudy at lunch time. I didn't bring an umbrella."

Peter turned to me. "I've got mine," he said softly. "We go the same way. I'll walk you."

"Thanks," I said. "I'd appreciate that."

"It's in Miss Krieter's cloakroom," he said. "I'll go get it. Wait for me by the front door."

By the time he joined me there, everyone else had gone. We walked out into the rain together. It was coming down hard, but straight, so his big black umbrella kept us dry and safe.

"Lucky you brought this," I said, "or we'd both have come down with the grippe."

"Thank my mother," he said. "I certainly wouldn't have brought it if she hadn't stood at the door and handed it to me as I left."

I laughed. "You surprise me, Peter. I thought you always did what you were supposed to do."

"And I thought you always did what you were supposed to," he retorted. "I guess we were both wrong."

"Why, what did I ever do that I wasn't supposed to do?" I asked.

"Teased Mr. Allison," he replied quickly. "Now was that nice?"

"Who started it, may I ask?" I answered haughtily. "Not me."

"It was you who made up the quotation," he said, "and its author."

"As the editor," I said, "you shouldn't let me do things like that."

"So neither of us is any good. Just like I said. 'Partners in crime.' Who said that?"

I shook my head. "I don't know."

The rain began to come down harder, and at an angle. Beneath the umbrella, we were beginning to get a bit damp.

"Let's go into the Candy Kitchen," he said, "until this passes over. I'll buy you a root beer."

"I can't," I said. "I've got to get home. I have to help Mama with dinner."

"Then another time," he said.

"Yes," I said. "Maybe."

"Well, which is it?" he asked. "Yes or maybe?"

"Oh, you know what I mean," I said. I was getting a little nervous.

"Can I buy you a root beer tomorrow?" he asked.

"Oh goodness no," I said hastily. "Certainly not tomorrow. I have to be home even earlier than usual tomorrow."

"Why?" he insisted.

"It's *shabbos*—our sabbath. I have to help Mama get ready for it."

"My God," he said, "do you people have nothing but holidays? Your religion takes up all your time!"

I didn't like that remark at all. It was hard to believe it came from the boy who'd been so sensitive about my missing a meeting because of Yom Kippur.

"I guess that's the general idea," I said dryly. I wanted him to know he'd made a mistake. "Then you don't have time to get into trouble."

"Having a root beer with me?" he asked. "Would that be getting into trouble?"

I blushed. "In a way," I said. "Oh come on, Peter, you know what I mean."

"For goodness sake, Becky," he said angrily, "all I want to do is buy you a root beer!"

We had reached our building now. I stopped by the entrance to the store. "I'll walk you around to the back," he said.

"No," I replied. "I'll go in through here. There're stairs in the store. They'll be quicker—and drier.

Thanks an awful lot," I said. "It was really swell of you to let me share your umbrella."

He shrugged. "It was nothing," he said shortly. If he had been a girl, I'd have said he was pouting. Peter van Ruysdaal was used to having his own way.

"Well, thanks again," I repeated lamely. "See you in school tomorrow."

"Yeah," he said. "So long."

I walked into the store, but through the window I could see him crossing the wet shiny street. I watched him until he had disappeared in the deepening twilight. Then I went upstairs.

"The meeting lasted a long time," Mama said as I entered the kitchen.

"Yes," I said, "but we got a lot done."

"I told you to take an umbrella at lunch time," she said. "You must be soaked. Go change your clothes." She looked at me carefully. "But you don't seem to be soaked."

"I don't need to change," I said. "I walked home under an umbrella."

"Oh?" Mama asked. "Whose umbrella?"

"Peter's," I said.

"Peter?" She raised her eyebrows, as if she didn't know who I was talking about.

"Peter van Ruysdaal," I said.

"You walked home under an umbrella with Peter van Ruysdaal?" Mama repeated.

"Mama," I pointed out patiently, "it was just to stay dry."

"I told your papa when we moved here," she said, "that this would happen. I'm surprised it didn't happen before this."

"That what would happen, Mama? Nothing has happened."

She ignored me. "We're lucky," she went on, "that your interests lie in other directions. Otherwise it surely would have happened before this."

"Mama, I walked home under an umbrella with Peter van Ruysdaal to keep dry. What are you trying to make out of that?"

"His mother won't like it any more than me," Mama warned. "Even less."

"Like what?" I said. "There's nothing to like or not like. Mama, this isn't the ghetto. Just because you say hello to a Christian doesn't mean the next step is conversion."

"Make your old mother happy," Mama said. "Find another umbrella next time."

"You get Ruth to help you with dinner," I said. "I'm not going to sit here and listen to this nonsense."

"You stay right here and help me, Miss," Mama ordered. "Ruth is at Carrie Kyle's house."

"Oh, that's all right," I said. "Ruth can talk to Christians. She doesn't have to live in the Middle Ages."

"Ruth is only twelve," Mama pointed out. "Besides, Carrie is a girl."

"She's got a fourteen-year-old brother," I retorted. "If I were you, Mama, I'd run right over there and drag her home before he molests her or something."

"Don't talk like that, Rifka," Mama said. "It's not nice."

I sighed. After a certain point, conversation with my mother just ran out. Her responses were all so automatic, the result of the handful of firmly set ideas that she carried around in her head. I could have really made her liver curl if I'd told her about the book of love poetry that Mr. Allison had given me to take to Annie Klein, but of course I didn't tell her.

Papa made a very perfunctory *kiddush* in the *sukkah* that night. Only Mama joined him. Ruth and I stayed inside. Mama allowed this because the rain might endanger our health. The only thing that took precedence in her mind over religious proprieties was health.

At dinner Mama told Papa all about my walk home with Peter and we covered the same ground again. Papa's manner often suggested that he was much more flexible than Mama, but in reality he was not. It was just that there were fewer issues on which he took an absolutist point of view. Jewish girls having anything at all to do with non-Jewish boys was one. I told them I wasn't having anything to do with a *"goy"*—a stranger—at least not in the way they meant. I pointed out that it would be ridiculous for me not to be on terms of normal friendship with the members of my class whom I had known since first grade.

"They're no friends of yours," Mama said ominously. "Don't forget that."

"This is not Russia," I said. "A pogrom is not going to break out tomorrow."

"What makes you so sure of that?" Mama asked. "For Jews, it's the same everywhere."

"You can't really believe that, Mama," I said. "Surely it has been different here."

"Leo Frank was lynched right here in the United States only two years ago," Mama reminded me.

But Papa agreed with me. Or at least he agreed with me more. "I honestly believe that was an isolated incident," he said. "Certainly it's different here. Anti-semitism is not official government policy. It's easier to make a living here. It's easier to get an education."

"But it's harder," Mama said, "to be a Jew."

"Mama," I cried, "I'm a Jew. I can't be anything else. I don't want to be anything else. But does that mean there has to be a wall between me and the rest of the world?"

"There is a wall between you and the rest of the world," Mama said. "It's already there."

"Well, then," I said, "maybe it should be torn down."

"You have a very short memory," Mama said to me. "Don't you remember the Friday I didn't feel well and I sent you to the rabbi's for the chicken?"

Remember? The incident was incised in my mind like writing on a stone. It happened the summer I was ten. The rabbi's house was near the railroad tracks, a little less than a mile east of the station. To get there I had to walk along a dusty, narrow dirt road lined with tumbledown, unpainted cottages. All along the street kids were outside, playing, if you could call it that. The girls were mostly screaming and the boys were throwing rocks at tin cans. It was a very hot day. I was starched and neat, though, in my blue and white checked dress and my stiff white pinafore. Mama would never let us out on the street dressed as these kids were— the boys only in their trousers, the girls only in their shifts.

I had to watch the rabbi kill the chicken, which was bad enough. But then, holding the thing by its scrawny neck, I had to carry it home. I had to carry it back down that dusty, unpaved street. The kids were waiting for me as I came out of the rabbi's gate.

"Jew," one of them screamed.

"Dirty Jew," another echoed.

A third picked up a rock, of which the road provided a more than adequate supply, and threw it at me.

I held my head high and continued to walk, looking neither to the right nor the left. There was really nothing else to do.

"Jew girl gonna eat the chicken."

"Jew girl gonna drink its blood."

Then the rocks started coming at me thick and fast. They were all throwing rocks. One hit my legs, another my shoulder. I began to run.

"Yellow Jew girl."

"Dirty yellow Jew."

Their screams and their rocks chased me down the block. I ran as fast as my legs would carry me. I ran all the way home, even though they did not follow me beyond their neighborhood, and once I was on the pavement, there was no longer any reason to run.

When I got home, sweaty and dirty, my starched

pinafore a limp and dusty ruin, the poor chicken still clutched in my hand, I sobbed my story out to my mother. She bathed me and gave me lemonade to drink and comforted me.

"Nasty *trombeniks*," she said. "Dirty little *goyim*. They're stupid. They're ignorant. You don't have to have anything to do with them. Forget all about it. Forget all about it now."

I had never forgotten about it, and neither had my mother. She never sent me for the chicken again, not even after I had grown up, and she never sent Ruthie either.

"But Mama," I said, remembering it all once more. "You missed the point. I wasn't crying just because those children had been mean to me. I was crying because I was so mad at myself. I was yellow, just like they said. I should have faced them."

"And gotten killed?" Mama said. "What are you, crazy? The only thing to do with *goyim* is stay away from them. Have as little to do with them as possible. If the Jews haven't learned anything else in two thousand years, they certainly should have learned that." Then she added, as if apropos of nothing, but of course it was apropos of everything, "Make sure you're home nice and early tomorrow. Henry Braude's coming for *shabbos* dinner."

"He is?" Papa asked.

"Yes," Mama replied firmly. "I'll call Moishe's store tomorrow and invite him."

The next morning, in school, I saw Peter hanging his black umbrella in Miss Krieter's cloakroom. The day looked like more rain. I decided to hang my umbrella on the hook next to his.

"I think I'd like a root beer," I said. "I think I'd like one very much. I'll get to the Candy Kitchen about four-thirty. I'll help my mother first."

"Good," he said. "Football practice'll be done by then. Come earlier if it rains."

I shook my head. "Four-thirty," I said. My heart was pounding, because however I tried to rationalize my actions, I knew I was deliberately defying my parents, in an action, not just in words. I hadn't done that since I was seven years old and had gone wading in van Zandt's brook one hot summer day, an activity which had been expressly and specifically forbidden. I had been spanked hard for that one. I could not remember deliberately disobeying my parents since then, though I had certainly been known to talk fresh, as my mother never tired of pointing out. However, all those years my mind had been going its own way. Sooner or later, that was bound to show.

Peter nodded. "Four-thirty," he agreed. Then we went our separate ways. We did not speak to each other for the rest of the day. Any other day we would have.

When the bell rang at three o'clock I rushed out of school as if the whole Russian army were after me. I had an awful lot to do in an hour and a half. First I ran over to Annie Klein's. I kind of hoped she wasn't home so that all I'd have to do was drop the books off with a note, but she was there, dutifully preparing her *shabbos* dinner. "We're going to eat home tonight, for once," she said. "The old lady will have to be satisfied with our making *kiddush* with them in the *sukkah*. But stay and keep me company while I cook, Becky. We can talk."

"I can't," I said. "I have to help Mama. I just brought these books over. Mr. Allison sent them."

"That was very nice of him. He's a nice man."

"I don't know how nice a man he is," I said. "What's he sending you books for?"

"You sound like your mother," Annie said. "Suspicious. He just wants to help me get educated. He's a teacher, after all."

"But these are love poems," I said. "What did he send you love poems for?"

"They are?" Annie smiled. "He didn't say that. He just asked me if I'd ever read any poetry by Elizabeth Barrett Browning, and I said I'd never even heard of her, and he said my education was sadly lacking and I agreed. So he said he'd lend me some books and maybe I could fill in the gaps on my own."

"He told me he'd answer any questions you might have when he met you in Cartland's Pharmacy," I said.

She smiled again, a self-satisfied little smile, but she said only, "When I'm done with the books you can take them back to him."

"Give them to him yourself," I said, "in Cartland's."

"I'm not going to carry them around just on the chance of running into him," she said.

"You're not?" I replied. "Well, that's something, anyway."

"You're so silly, Becky," Annie said. "It's just as I said. You're getting more and more like your mother every day." I shook my head. That particular day I couldn't believe I was anything like my mother at all. "But I love you anyway," Annie went on. "Come back soon. I'm going to need company. Sid's going away for two months."

"What!" I was really surprised. "For two months! Why? Where?"

"He's going to Poland," Annie said, "to bring back his aunt."

"Can't she come herself? Why does he have to go for her?"

"No one knows where she is," Annie said. "The last couple of letters have come back unopened, and when Papa Klein wrote to some people he knew in the old village, they said his sister went to Warsaw a year ago and no one's heard a thing from her since. No one even knows her address in Warsaw. She just told them she was going to visit some cousins, and then she disappeared. But there are no cousins in Warsaw. At least none Papa Klein knows about. He's too sick to go look for her himself, so he's sending Sid. He's worried she's gone crazy or something. She lost her only daughter and her three grandchildren in a fire two years ago. Papa Klein begged her to come then, but she wouldn't. It's a terrible situation, and I know Sid has to go, but I wish he didn't. There's a war going on over there. Anything can happen!"

I felt sick to my stomach. In addition to the danger

of traveling to Europe at that time, it seemed to me very unfortunate that Sid had to leave Annie just now. She was not the sort who liked being alone. It would have been better if she had a baby. "I'll come to see you," I assured her. "I'll come as often as I can. Everyone will. You know that."

"Yes," Annie said. "Especially the old lady!"

"Well, then, you come to our house," I said, "so you won't be home when she comes creaking up the stairs."

Annie hugged me. "You're a good friend, Becky Levitsky," she said. "You understand a lot of things."

"Well, maybe," I said. I glanced at her kitchen clock. It was nearly three-thirty. "Look, I've got to go now," I said. "Try not to worry. Two months isn't so long. He could be back by Chanukah." I kissed her and left quickly. I was worried about her, but I pushed it to the back of my mind. I had too many other things to think about.

It was just a couple of minutes after three-thirty when I got home, and for an hour I helped Mama. I was a veritable whirlwind. I worked faster than I had ever worked in my life. I made the *matzoh* balls for the chicken soup. Mama said mine were lighter than hers. I made a noodle pudding too. But when the clock read 4:25 I said to Mama, "Let Ruth set the table. I'm going out for a little while."

"Out?" Mama asked. "Where?"

"To the Candy Kitchen," I said, "for a root beer."

"Friday afternoon? All of a sudden? Why?"

"I've done my work," I said. "Everyone's there.

They're all there on Friday afternoon. Lilly Cohen and Abe Greenbaum too." I couldn't lie to her about where I was going. There was no hiding anything in Winter Hill. But I didn't mention Peter. When she found out about that, let her think it was an accident. "I'll be back by five-thirty," I went on. "Candle lighting isn't until six. I'll be back in plenty of time."

"Is this going to be every Friday?" Mama asked.

"Oh, I don't know," I said. "But they're my friends, and they asked me to come."

"Go ahead," she said, sighing. For years she had been complaining that I read too much, that I'd ruin my health cooped up all my days with a book, that I should get out and have some fun with people my own age. Now that I was planning to do just that, it was hard for her to refuse me since it was only Lilly Cohen and Abe Greenbaum. I prayed they really would be there. It was not unlikely. What I had said about everyone showing up at the Candy Kitchen on a Friday afternoon was true enough. I threw in the clincher. "If Henry comes early," I said, "send him down to get me."

"All right," Mama said. "Go ahead. Ruth is playing on the street. Send her up."

"It'll be good for her to help," I said. "She gets away with murder. It's time she had a few responsibilities around here. Why should all the work fall on me?"

"In a kitchen," Mama said, "Ruth is like a bull in a china shop."

"She ought to start learning sometime," I said.

Mama nodded. "Maybe you're right," she said. "Send her up. Go ahead."

I left. But by the time I found Ruth and sent her upstairs I realized it must be quarter of five. Perhaps Peter had gotten tired of waiting and gone home. I began to run. Then I decided I didn't want to arrive all hot and sweaty and over-eager. I had a little pride. I slowed down to a fast walk.

Peter was still there. There were only a few tables in the Candy Kitchen. He and Dick and Mabel and Isabel and two or three others were sitting at one of them. He stood up when I walked in the door. A big grin broke out over his face. It seemed as if he had given me up, and now that I had come, my arrival was an unexpected pleasure.

"Becky," he called, "over here. Come sit with us."

I walked over to his table. Abe and Lilly were in the candy store too. They were at another table. But they were sitting with a whole bunch of juniors like themselves. I smiled at them as I went by, but really, I told myself, no one could be surprised that I didn't sit with them.

I joined Peter and the others. Peter got up and went over to the counter and got me a root beer. I sat next to him, drinking it, but I didn't say much. The conversation was mostly about the game the next day and whether Winter Hill had a chance of defeating Bloomsbury High.

"You going to be there?" Peter turned to me. "You going to be there to cheer us on?" He meant cheer *me* on. I knew that's what he meant, because he held my eyes as he asked me.

I turned away and began playing with my glass. "No," I said softly, "I can't come."

"Ah, why not?" Wally Buford said. "It'll probably be the best game of the season. You wouldn't want to miss the sight of old Wally kicking a field goal would you?"

"Can it, Wally," Dick said, "you've never kicked one yet. Why should tomorrow be any different?"

"I feel it," Wally said. "Tomorrow is a new beginning for Wally Buford. Wait 'til I get to Rutgers. You'll be sorry you made fun of me when you read in the papers how I scored the winning touchdown against Princeton." Dick only raised his eyebrows.

"You see?" Peter said. "You see what's in store for you? You have to come."

"I can't," I said. I felt a kind of lump in my throat and I couldn't speak very loud. "It's our sabbath. We can't do things like going to ball games on our sabbath."

"Oh, phooey," Mabel said. "Methodists aren't supposed to dance, but I'm a Methodist and I dance. You work in the store on Saturday. I've seen you there."

"I do if Papa needs me," I said. My voice was stronger now. Why should Mabel or anyone else, even Peter, make me feel apologetic about what my family —and I—believed in? "We have to make a living," I said. "Mama doesn't like it, though she puts up with it. But she'd never allow me to go to a football game on Saturday."

"Solly's on the team," Peter pointed out.

"Solly's mother has different ideas than my mother," I said. "Just like I guess Mabel's mother has different ideas than some other Methodist mothers."

"What my mother doesn't know won't hurt her," Mabel said with a giggle.

"It's hard to keep secrets in Winter Hill," I said.

"If you come to the game tomorrow," Peter said, "none of us will tell. You can count on that."

"Tell your mother you're going to visit your cute friend," Mabel said. "I'm sure she won't tell either."

"What cute friend?" I asked. "Who are you talking about?"

"You know the one I mean," Mabel said. "The one Mr. Allison likes."

"Mabel, what are you talking about?" I repeated. I knew perfectly well what she was talking about.

"I see them in Cartland's Pharmacy whenever I go in, and I'm there a lot," Mabel said. "I'm always buying Sedlitz powders for my grandmother. She has a terrible lot of gas."

"Oh," I said as casually as I could, "I guess you mean Annie Klein. She has to buy a lot of medicine for her father-in-law. He's sickly."

"But who is Mr. Allison buying medicine for?" Mabel asked archly. "He looks healthy as a horse and he lives alone in a room in Mrs. Coomb's boarding house."

I laughed a little nervously. "You see what I mean when I say you can't keep a secret in Winter Hill?"

Then I thought, "How dare she make insinuations about Annie?" I shook my head and said firmly, "Anyway, I don't want to go to the game tomorrow. I wouldn't go even if I could." I wondered what had gotten into me. I was contrary with my mother; I was contrary with my classmates. I couldn't seem to decide whose side I was on. I was on the opposite side of whomever I was with.

"Tomorrow afternoon," I went on, "we're going to take a *sukkah* walk."

"A what?" Isabel asked.

"A *sukkah* walk," I explained. "We're in the middle now of a harvest holiday called Sukkos. The Pilgrims read about it in the Bible and that's where they got the idea for Thanksgiving. We're supposed to build these little booths now and take our meals in them for a week. Tomorrow some of us are going to visit our friends and have a glass of wine in their huts. I wouldn't want to miss it. It's fun," I added defiantly.

"Well," Isabel shrugged, "to each his own."

"At least you get a lot of wine that way," Dick added.

"Yeah," I agreed. No one said anything else so I got up. "Well, I guess I'd better be going now," I said. "It's late." I turned to Peter. "Thanks for the root beer."

He shrugged. "That's O.K.," he said. He did not offer to see me home. I would have turned him down if he had, but I was annoyed that he hadn't offered. I walked out of the Candy Kitchen without looking back. It had been a mistake. The whole thing had been a mistake. Mama was right. They were not really friends of mine. None of them. They did not understand.

I tried at dinner to be as pleasant as I could to Henry, but it was hard. Sometimes my mind wandered from the conversation at the table, and I was lost in my own thoughts. I had Annie to worry about; I had to figure out why Peter had asked me to the Candy Kitchen in the first place. I had to figure out why I thought my mother an idiot one minute and agreed with her totally the next.

"Still dreaming, Miss Rebecca?" Henry asked me. "Still lost in your own world?"

His remark, uttered practically in my ear, but hardly in a whisper, called me back to the table. "Becky does that lots," Ruthie said. "Lots of times she doesn't seem to be here at all."

"A person is entitled to his private thoughts, Ruth," Papa reprimanded her.

"I hope she's agreed to work for you when she graduates," Henry said to Papa. "I hope you've talked her out of her silly ideas."

Papa took umbrage at Henry's remark. "Rebecca will do as she's told," he said. "But she can have any ideas she wants to have," he said. "It's a free country. As I just told Ruth a person is entitled to his thoughts." Maybe Papa was beginning to have doubts about Henry Braude as a candidate for my hand.

Not so Mama. She beamed at him as he joined us, after the table had been cleared, in singing sabbath songs. He had a fine, light baritone voice. I complimented him on it.

He nodded. "There's no point in doing a thing," he said, "unless you do it well."

No matter what he said, it set my teeth on edge. "We sing for fun," I said, "or to praise God. I'm sure God doesn't care about the quality of our voices."

"You persist in misunderstanding me, Miss Rebecca . . ." Henry began.

"Just call me Becky," I said. "Everyone else does. Except Mama, sometimes."

"What does she call you?" he asked.

"Rifka," I replied. Rifka is my Hebrew name.

Henry smiled. "I'd like to call you Rifka," he said.

There he goes again, I thought. I had not given him permission to use Mama's pet name for me. But I didn't say anything about it. I really was trying to be nice; at least for me I was.

There was no *sukkah* walk the next day. It rained all afternoon, most of which I spent staring gloomily out of the window. The rain cut down on business and Papa didn't even need me in the store. But the football game was played anyway. Winter Hill won, 16–7. It was the mud that did it. Bloomsbury was not good in the mud. Wally Buford did kick a field goal. And Peter van Ruysdaal scored a touchdown.

I found that all out when I went to school on Monday. Peter cornered me in the cloakroom and told me. I congratulated him.

"Thanks," he said. I detected a note of sarcasm in his voice, though I don't think there had been one in mine. "You left the Candy Kitchen awful fast Friday," he said. "What was the matter?"

"I just got the feeling," I began, "well . . . I just got the feeling I didn't really belong there. Maybe I should have sat at the table with Lilly and Abe."

"Lord, you're sensitive, Becky," he said. "You see insults everywhere, don't you?"

Unaccountably, I felt tears rising to the back of my eyes. I fought them down and managed to say, "Perhaps I just don't have your self-confidence. If I don't, it's for good reason. And if you want to know what I think, Peter," I continued bravely, "I don't think you're sensitive *enough*. None of you."

Peter nodded thoughtfully. "Maybe you're right," he said. "Don't be mad at me, Becky. Please don't be mad at me."

Now a tear did trickle down my cheek, but I smiled. "I'm not mad at you," I said. "How could I be mad at you?"

"I'm glad," Peter said. With his finger he touched the wet spot on my cheek. "I like you an awful lot, Becky. I really do."

He said it right out loud. And there were other boys and girls in and out of the cloakroom the whole time we were having this conversation. But I don't think they heard. We weren't exactly shouting. I was so overwhelmed by what he had said that I could only put my hand over my mouth and stare at him. "You look so surprised," he said. "Why? I thought lately I'd made it pretty clear."

"Me?" I finally managed to say. "Why me?"

"I don't know." Peter laughed. "Does a person have to have a reason? You're different, that's all."

I had no time to think of a reply. Suddenly Miss Krieter appeared at the cloakroom door. "I hate to interrupt your little tête-à-tête," she said sarcastically, "but the bell did ring. No doubt you were too engrossed to hear it."

I could feel a hot blush suffuse my whole face. I hurried out of that cloakroom as quickly as I could, mumbling a low apology to Miss Krieter as I passed her.

But Peter was much more self-possessed than I. "I am sorry, Miss Krieter," I heard him say firmly as he came out behind me, "but Rebecca and I were so busy talking about the annual we're putting together that we just didn't pay any attention to anything else." He said it loud enough for the whole class to hear. But Isabel wasn't fooled. She turned around and stared at me frowningly as I took my seat. She had more or less gone around with Peter the previous year, and I guess she thought she was going around with him still.

Oh, lord, I thought, the fat's in the fire now. But deep down inside of me there was a core of secret pleasure at the notion that Peter van Ruysdaal liked me. Because I liked him. I always had. Who wouldn't? In our high school you would have had to be blind, deaf, and dumb not to like Peter van Ruysdaal.

Chanukah

AT FIRST, nothing came of it. I was much too nervous to let anything come of it. If my mother found out her suspicions about me and Peter were true, I couldn't even begin to imagine what she'd do. Or I could imagine it. That was the trouble. She'd probably push me under the wedding canopy with Henry Braude at gunpoint and I wouldn't even be allowed to finish high school.

I patiently explained all this to Peter. We began to have lunch-time meetings of the annual staff because too many of the boys were involved in after-school athletics to make meetings at three very profitable. I brought my lunch to school in a brown paper bag every day now, even if it wasn't raining, and even if we didn't have a meeting. So did Peter. We sat in the back of Mr. Allison's empty classroom, eating and talking. We had tried Miss Krieter's room, but she kept making conversation. Mr. Allison left us alone. He had his own problems.

Lunch in the back of Mr. Allison's room was all that we had. We didn't go anywhere together. I wouldn't walk home with him. I wouldn't meet him again in the Candy Kitchen on a Friday afternoon. I wouldn't go to football games. I explained it all to him. I explained how my parents felt. "But I'm not asking you to marry me," Peter said. "I'm just asking you to let me walk home with you."

"Peter," I said patiently, for the four hundred and seventieth time, "they don't understand that."

"But you do," he said.

"I won't upset them that way," I said. "I can't do it. Besides, who knows to what extremes they might go? They might say I can't come to school anymore. Let's just eat lunch together," I went on. "Let's just keep it this way. You can walk Isabel home. You can take Isabel to parties. We can just be friends and talk."

The petulant look I was growing accustomed to appeared on his face. "I don't want to walk home with Isabel," he said. "I don't want to take Isabel to parties. If you're not there, I don't want to go to the stupid parties. I'm sick of them. They're so boring."

"Well, you'd better go," I said. "Christmas is coming, and there'll be lots of them." Every year Peter and his sister, Amelia, had a Christmas party, and before them, their older brother, Dirck, had had a Christmas party. It was a tradition in the van Ruysdaal family that the young people entertain during Christmas week. It was the party that everyone wanted to go to. "If you don't do your usual things, your mother's going to wonder why," I said. "And I know that your mother wouldn't like the idea of us together any more than my mother!"

"I don't believe that," Peter said.

"Don't you? Then why don't you ask her?"

"What's the point of discussing an abstraction?" he said. "I've got a better idea. You come to my Christmas party. Let her meet you."

"She's met me," I said.

"I mean get to know you," Peter insisted. "Not from behind a counter."

"I can't come," I said. "Even if your mother said

that it was all right for me to come, my mother wouldn't let me go."

He ignored me. "I'll invite Solly, too," he said. "He's on the team so I know him, even though he's only a sophomore. Melie can invite Abe and Lilly." They were in her class.

I looked at him thoughtfully. If the others were going too, then maybe Mama would let me go. "Well," I said in a small voice, "we can try."

"And will you invite me to your house during Christmas?" he asked.

"We don't celebrate Christmas," I said.

"Oh, I know that," he replied. "I know you don't go to church or anything like that. But Christmas is such a general celebration—sort of an American holiday, like the Fourth of July . . ."

"I'm not a Christian," I said. "Only Christians celebrate Christmas. Did you know that more than half the world is not Christian? Did you know that Peter?"

"I think these religious differences are all silly," Peter said. "We're all the same underneath. We're all Americans. I think the day will come when we'll all be the same religion, and the world will be a much better place for it."

"And what religion will that be?" I asked.

"Oh, I don't know. Some mixture, I guess."

"Well, it sounds peaceful," I said. "But sort of bland. Do you think you'd really like it if we were all the same? It would be like an orchestra with nothing in it but violins."

"Well, maybe we could each stay our own religion,"

Peter said, "only we should emphasize the samenesses, not the differences." This was what I enjoyed so much about our lunches together—these long philosophical discussions. There was no one else I could have them with, and I don't think there was anyone else Peter could have them with either. We talked about everything—whether women would get the vote, whether Theodore Roosevelt would—or should—run again, whether the United States would be drawn into the war raging in Europe, whether Winston Churchill or Booth Tarkington was the better novelist, whether Princeton would defeat Rutgers in their annual football game again that year. We disagreed on almost every one of those subjects but, lord, how we enjoyed wrangling over them. We enjoyed the crackling tension between us. We enjoyed the exercise our minds were getting. It was better than the debating team which that year was taking up the topic, "Resolved that the United States government should own and operate telegraphs and telephones within its borders."

By December, New Jersey had defeated women's suffrage in a special election. Princeton had defeated Rutgers at football as they had regularly since 1869. The United States had not been pulled into the war—not yet. Sid Klein, contrary to my hopes, was not back from Poland by Chanukah. And my mother had at last consented to my going to Peter's Christmas party. Her consent was wrung from her unwillingly. I had persisted. I brought the subject up every single afternoon while we were making supper. The conversation was always the same.

"I don't see why you won't let me go to the van Ruysdaals' Christmas party," I always said.

"A Jewish girl doesn't belong at a Christmas party," she always replied.

"Oh, Mama, don't be ridiculous. No one's going to say any prayers or anything. Christmas is just an excuse for having a party."

"There's no reason for you to go to a party in a *goyishe* house any time."

"Solly's going. Abe and Lilly are going."

"If their parents don't care what happens to them," Mama answered firmly, "that's not my business. But you are my business."

I was getting nowhere, so I turned to Lilly. I asked her to come into the store and talk to my parents. Papa liked Lilly, who was, if anything, even prettier than Annie Klein. She came in on a busy Saturday. Mama and I were both there, helping. Mama would show material, patterns, and notions to the customers, but she wouldn't cut cloth from bolts and she wouldn't take money. There was a limit to how far she could go in desecrating the sabbath.

"Mr. Levitsky," Lilly said to my father as she handed him a dime for two spools of thread, "why won't you let Becky go to the van Ruysdaals' party?" She avoided the word "Christmas." "Everyone's going."

"Becky doesn't have to do what everyone is doing," my mother said firmly.

Lilly was not discouraged. She ignored my mother and smiled at my father as she reached out her hand and touched his sleeve. "You know," she said, "it's really quite an honor to have been invited. It shows that we're really accepted here in Winter Hill. It shows we're really part of the town now."

Papa looked at Mama. "Let her go," he said. "It wouldn't be nice for her to refuse. It would look bad. They make a gesture to us, we shouldn't reject it."

"But Chaim . . ." Mama began.

He turned and looked at her. "It would be bad for business. Mrs. van Ruysdaal's a very good customer. Let Becky go."

And so it was settled. Afterwards I thanked Lilly. She knew all about me and Peter, of course. He and I were still eating lunch together every day. All our friends knew about us, but they didn't say anything— at least not to us, or to any grown-up. I don't know what they were saying to each other. Isabel Liebig had stopped speaking to me altogether.

Since it was now arranged that I was to come to his house, Peter was growing more insistent that he come to mine. I think he really believed that if my mother met him, she'd give some kind of stamp of approval to our relationship. He knew he was hard to resist. But he didn't know my mother. I sometimes thought I ought to let him come, just so he'd realize what a hard nut she was, and stop bothering me about it. But the occasion would have been so unpleasant that I couldn't have borne it. He couldn't believe that in the whole month of December there wasn't going to be some kind of celebration in my house during which he could sort of sneak in unobserved. He had finally come to understand that we really didn't mark Christmas in any way whatsoever, but he said, "You have some kind of holiday in December. I know you do. You've got holidays all the rest of the time."

"Only Chanukah in December," I said. "We light candles every night for eight days to mark an ancient victory. Papa gives Ruth and me money. It's just a minor festival. A family festival. No big parties. Not like Passover when we have this monstrous dinner that lasts all night."

"Maybe I can come then."

"Maybe," I said. I felt safe saying that. Passover wasn't until the spring, by which time Peter might have gotten tired of our paper-bag relationship and gone back to Isabel or found someone else. I wasn't looking forward to that day, and yet I regarded it as inevitably arriving pretty soon. He wasn't going to be content with sharing apples and Tootsie Rolls forever, and I think if it was not for the fact that he took as much pleasure in what we had to say to each other as I did, he'd have dropped the whole thing a long time before as the inexplicable fancy of the moment. After all, since sixth grade, when he'd first noticed girls, he'd gone through practically everyone in the class. I had been about the only one left.

After school that day I dropped by Annie's. She was making me a dress for the party and she wanted me to try it on. Besides I had another book for her from Mr. Allison. It was not a loan, but a gift, because it was wrapped in fancy paper. When Annie opened it, I saw that it was Tennyson's *Idylls of the King*. I thought that a much better choice than Elizabeth Browning, until I watched her blush as she turned to the flyleaf.

"What does it say?" I asked.

"Nothing," she replied quickly, slamming it shut.

"Come on, Annie," I said. "It's a gift, it's got to say something."

She handed it to me silently. I opened it up. "To Guinevere," it read, in Mr. Allison's elaborate Spencerian hand, "from Lancelot." I dropped it on the table as if it was hot. "What are you going to do with it," I asked with heavy irony, "when Sid comes home?"

"Sometimes I think Sid's never coming home," Annie said sadly. "I'm so lonesome I can't stand it."

I thought of our mothers and grandmothers separated for years at a time from their husbands who had often come to America ahead of them to earn money for the rest of the family's passage. Annie had never known any hardship or difficulty. Much as I loved her, I had to admit that she was very spoiled.

"Now that he knows his aunt is dead," I said, "he's bound to be home soon."

"There are so many loose ends to tie up," she replied. "That's what he says. Everything's complicated a thousand times by the war. It's all a big mess." She picked Mr. Allison's book up off the table. "I'm throwing this out, of course," she said. "He had no right to say anything like that to me. I've certainly never encouraged him to regard me as anything more than a student."

"I can't blame him," I said, "for thinking that meeting him twice a week in the drug store is encouragement." It was the talk of the town.

"That's an accident," she said. "It's a public place. He can come in whenever he wants."

"You'd better start buying your tooth powder on different days," I said. "Even the kids at school mentioned it to me."

"I don't care," Annie insisted. "Sid's off in Europe, in the middle of a war and I'm stuck here in Winter Hill where nothing ever happens. I've got to talk to someone, or I'll go out of my mind."

"You've got me," I said. "You've got all your friends."

"Oh, pooh!" Annie said. "What fun are they? I don't mean you," she added hastily. "But the others . . . stick-in-the-muds, every one of them. At least Ken . . . Mr. Allison . . . knows something. At least he can talk about something!"

"Please, Annie," I begged, "don't do anything foolish."

"Oh, honey," Annie said with a laugh, "what can I do in the middle of Cartland's Pharmacy, with Doc Cartland staring at me the whole time? Poor Ken—he can't even give me a book in the drug store because of that. He has to send it home with you. At least we give people in this hick town something to talk about. They ought to thank us. It won't come to anything. Any more than you and Peter will come to anything."

"Who told you about that?" I asked.

"Ken," she replied. "He says you and Peter eat lunch together in the back of his room almost every day."

"Well," I said, "I guess that's it. Mama'll never let me go to his party now." I felt almost relieved.

"I'm not telling your Mama anything," Annie said. "You don't talk about me, I don't talk about you. Come on. Let's try on the dress. When he sees you in that, Mr. Peter van Ruysdaal is going to go out of his mind."

"I hope not," I cried. I'd had some trouble with Annie over the dress. Originally she had wanted to make me the evening gown in *Vogue* magazine that she had shown me several months before. Some instinct warned me that such a dress in the van Ruysdaal house would be a disaster. I knew I had to dress in the style of the Baumgartner and Goldberg ladies. I finally persuaded her to make me a simple gown in a rose net lace with wide elbow-length sleeves, a triple flounced skirt, and a wide girdle of deep-rose velvet. She did convince me that the bodice did not have to come up to my neck, but might be properly rounded off somewhere well below the collarbone.

I tried it on in Annie's bedroom in front of her full-length mirror. Annie sat on the floor and pinned up the hem, while I watched myself in fascination. With my dark hair, dark eyes, and fresh complexion, the rose color was perfect. Even I could see that.

"I love it, Annie," I cried. "I just love it. Thank you so much for making it for me. It makes me feel like a princess."

"The right dress can do that," Annie said. "I'm so glad you feel that way. I still like the other one better, but if you had felt uncomfortable in it, it would never have done." She stood up, pincushion and skirt marker in hand. "Take it off now so I can do the hem."

"Oh, I'll do that," I said. "You've gone to enough trouble." I hugged her. "Annie, why should you be so good to me? I can't thank you enough."

"You're my friend, Becky," she said simply. She smiled at me for a moment and then she added, "But you certainly will not hem this dress. I finish what I start. Do you think for one second I'd let you put your clumsy stitches in this lovely piece of lace? Now, take it off before you crush it!"

"Come home and have supper with us," I said after I had stopped being a princess and become an ordinary schoolgirl in a white shirtwaist and a blue serge skirt. I did not like the picture I had in my mind of Annie lighting her two Chanukah candles—it was the second night of the holiday—all by herself and probably not even eating a proper dinner. I knew her mother-in-law would have asked her downstairs and I knew also she'd have asked in such a way that Annie would have found refusing a pleasure.

I could see Annie liked the idea. "But your mother . . ." she began.

"My mother will be pleased to see you." My mother had never been much of a fan of Annie Klein's, but when Mrs. Ginsberg had passed a remark about Annie's drug store conversations with Mr. Allison, Mama had replied, "Sid had no business to leave her like this—a new bride of less than a year. The old man should have sent his brother from Pittsburgh. If you ask me, Bessie's in back of the whole thing." Bessie was

Sid's mother. "It would have been better if Annie had gone to stay with her folks in Newark while Sid was away."

"Her stepmother didn't want her," I said. "Annie told me her stepmother was glad when she got married and moved out. There's only one bedroom in their apartment, and three children."

"She should have gone anyway," Mama said. "It would have been better." I had an idea Mama was right. It was too bad Annie's mother had died in the old country. Annie's stepmother was rather young herself and not very interested in a strikingly handsome twenty-year-old stepdaughter. What Annie really didn't have, anywhere, was someone to be a mother to her, and I knew that for all of her disapproval of some of the things Annie did, my mother would welcome her for supper.

As indeed she did. "I hope it's no trouble, Mrs. Levitsky," Annie said with her charming smile. "Becky just insisted. But I know you weren't expecting me and if you don't have enough, I can go back."

"Not have enough?" Mama was insulted. "Here, there's always enough, thank God. All I have to do is grate another potato." Mama was frying *latkes*, pancakes made out of grated raw potato and onion, and served with applesauce, sour cream, or jam. They are the most delicious things in the world and why they are associated with the holiday of Chanukah I can't imagine. In ancient days they certainly didn't eat them. They didn't even have potatoes in those days.

Papa drew Annie into the great Levitsky family debate. "Do you like your *latkes* smooth," he asked, "or hairy?"

"Hairy?" Annie asked in amazement.

"That means coarsely grated," Mama said. "That's how Mr. Levitsky likes them."

"When I was little, Bubbie and Zadie visited us one Chanukah," Ruthie explained. Bubbie and Zadie were my mother's parents. "Bubbie made *latkes*," Ruth went on, "but they were all smooth, so I said I liked my Mama's *latkes* better because they were hairy."

Annie laughed. "I guess I like hairy *latkes* too," she said.

Papa beamed. "One more for our side," he said to Mama.

Before we ate the pancakes, we lit the candles in the Chanukah menorah which Mama had placed on a table in front of the window. After we recited the blessings, we sang.

> Rock of Ages, let our song
> Praise Thy saving power.
> Thou amidst the raging storm
> Was't our sheltering tower.
> Furious they assailed us,
> But Thy arm availed us,
> And Thy word broke their sword
> When our own strength failed us.

Papa gave Ruth and me a quarter. He gave one to Annie too. When she protested he laid his hand on her arm. "For tonight," he said, "you're also my daughter."

Mama nodded in agreement and Annie looked as if she might cry.

It had begun to snow. Great white flakes were falling out of the sky and melting as soon as they hit the pavement. I walked Annie home under Papa's big black umbrella. The streets were dark and quiet. No one was out on foot and only a couple of horse and buggies and one or two autos passed us by. We walked quickly and in silence. It was damp and raw, not a night to saunter. But when we got to the Kleins' house, Annie said, "I had such a lovely evening. I haven't had such a nice night since Sid went away."

"He'll be home soon, Annie," I said. "I know he will. Come back and have supper with us again tomorrow night."

"Oh, Becky," she said, laughing, "I can't have supper with you every night. I shall have to do something else to keep myself busy until Sid comes home." She kissed me on the cheek. "Good night, dear friend," she said, and ran quickly up the steps into her house.

"Good night," I called after her. The snow had changed; the flakes were smaller now. They fell more thickly and had begun to stick to the ground. I wrapped my scarf tighter around my neck and trudged down Queen Street and then Main Street to the light and warmth of my home.

Peter's party was on the Sunday night after Christmas. It had really snowed a lot and though the streets and sidewalks had finally been cleared, I had to wear rubber overshoes over my beautiful new pumps. It was a walk of at least a mile to the van Ruysdaals' handsome yellow stucco house, with its barn and stables, on the outskirts of town. Living above the store as we did, Papa kept neither carriage nor automobile. Not that he couldn't afford one. There was just no place to house it. If he needed a carriage, he hired one from Kennan's Livery Stable and Garage, and he certainly did not regard my going to Peter's party as sufficient occasion for that. Solly Gershorn's father was in the scrap business, and he'd offered to pick Abe, Lilly, and me up in his wagon and drive us over, but we politely declined. We all agreed that walking would be better than appearing in a junk dealer's open wagon. It was good enough for us in the late summer filled with hay, but we didn't feature it when we were dressed in our best.

We walked over, the four of us together. We were nervous and needed each other to keep our spirits up. None of us except Lilly had ever been inside the van Ruysdaal house, and Lilly had been there only twice, to Amelia's birthday parties years ago. Once Amelia had entered seventh grade and started having boys to her parties, Lilly had no longer been invited.

The house was ablaze with lights. Several automobiles were parked in the circular drive. Peter had said that cousins from New Brunswick would come over for the party. We turned the doorbell crank, and a red-headed maid who looked younger than I opened the door. She took our wraps and overshoes and carried them away up the long flight of stairs that led to the bedrooms.

We stepped gingerly into the front parlor. It seemed to me that a hundred people filled the room, and another hundred the back parlor, which I could see because the double doors between the two rooms had been thrown open. I could not see Peter anywhere. Amelia was there, though, and she led Solly and Abe and Lilly off to the couch where some of their classmates were seated. I stood against the wall for a few moments, gazing at the gorgeously decorated Christmas tree next to the fireplace in which a gas fire burned brightly. Pine boughs filled the mantel, and a sprig of mistletoe hung in the wide double doorway between the front and back parlors. I did not know exactly what to do or where to go, when suddenly Dick appeared at my side.

"Becky," he said, "do you want something to eat? There're sandwiches and cookies and things in the dining room."

"Where's Peter?" I asked.

Dick shrugged. "I don't know—around here someplace. Come on, we'll get something."

I followed him back into the front hall and then into the dining room. "How about eggnog?" Dick asked. I had never had eggnog. I wasn't even sure what it was, but I nodded. Dick scooped some frothy white liquid out of a punch bowl and into a little cup and handed it to me. It was delicious—sweet and sharp at the same time, and it tickled my nose. "Don't drink it too fast," Dick warned. "It's got rum in it."

"Be a darling, Dick," a woman's voice said, "and

give me some too." Dick filled another cup and handed it to the lady standing next to me. She was dressed very smartly in a sheath gown of ice-blue satin with a short train. The over tunic of blue georgette had a draped bodice edged at the low oval neckline and short wide sleeves with yellow marabou, which also bordered the flared hem. A narrow belt of silver fabric and long white kid gloves completed her ensemble. Her hair was very flat and smooth, parted in the middle and held in place with a headband fitted tightly over her forehead and decorated with a cluster of egret feathers. I had never seen anyone dressed like that before in real life. Only in the movies or Annie's fashion magazines.

I guess I was staring at her. She smiled at me and held out her hand. "I'm Sally Carruthers," she said. "I'm Alice van Ruysdaal's sister. I don't think I've seen you here before."

I shook her proffered hand. "No," I said, "I'm Rebecca Levitsky. I'm a classmate of Peter's. I've never been here before." Her open, easy, almost masculine manner had put me at my ease. "You don't live in Winter Hill," I said. It was a statement, not a question. "You must be one of the New Brunswick relatives."

She took the cup of eggnog that Dick was holding out for her. "I grew up in New Brunswick," she said, "but after college I moved to New York. That's where I live now."

"College," I said. "You went to college?"

"Yes," she said with a smile. "Does that surprise you?"

"Not many girls go to college," I replied. "Not one

girl in our senior class is planning on it. There are a few who are thinking about normal school, but not one who is thinking about college!"

"That's kind of stupid, isn't it?" Sally said. I thought of her as Sally right away. She seemed to belong to my generation, not Mrs. van Ruysdaal's. "After all," she went on, "about all high school does is prepare you for college."

"I wish Becky could go instead of me," Dick said gloomily. "She's the smartest one in our class—except for Peter of course."

"What *are* you going to do when you graduate?" Sally asked. Her tone suggested it was not a casual question. She really wanted to know.

"My father thinks I'm going to work in his store. My mother thinks I'm going to marry Henry Braude. I don't want to do either. I don't want to do either, in the worst way. But I don't know what I do want to do!" There was something about Sally Carruthers that made me say things to her I hadn't said to Mabel, who'd been my friend for twelve years, or to Peter, with whom I daily discussed the problems of the world.

"Come, let's sit down," Sally said. "We'll talk about it. You'll excuse us, won't you, Dick?"

"Oh, sure," he said. "Peter just told me to watch out for Becky and make sure she got something to eat when she came in. I'll go find Isabel now." He was glad to be relieved of his responsibility. It never ceased to amaze me that Dick did whatever Peter told him to do.

"Let's sit right here," Sally said. The dining-room chairs had been lined up against the wall so that people could get to the table easily. "It's too crowded in the parlors. What a crush. Every year it seems to get worse."

We sat down. "Every year perhaps Peter and Amelia have more friends," I suggested.

"And a good thing too," Sally replied. "Most of the old ones are growing up to be just as stuffy as their parents." She smiled to take the sting out of her words, and for a fleeting moment she reminded me of Annie. Like her, she was fair and plump and pretty. But there was no look of discontent around her mouth or in her eyes.

"Do you live in New York with your husband?" I asked. The openness of her manner made it easy for me to ask her questions, even personal ones.

"Oh, I'm not married," she said. "I live in New York because that's where I work."

"What do you do?" I asked.

"I work for the New York *American*," she said.

"Are you a typist?" I asked.

She shook her head.

"Bookkeeper? Telephone operator?"

She laughed out loud. "I'm a reporter," she said. "What's commonly called a sob sister. I interview the mother of the murderer who's just been condemned to death. Soon I hope they'll let me near the hard news."

"Oh," I sighed, "I wish I could think of something like that to do. But of course, Papa would never let me."

"What do you like?" she asked. "I mean, what subjects do you like best?"

"I like languages," I said. "And English literature. I want to study Greek and Latin."

"You could translate," she said. "You could edit. You could teach. And if you decide to study modern languages too, there are even more things you can do. But you'd have to go to college. If you're as smart as Dick says you are, then you really have to go to college. Not that getting the right kind of position is so easy. You have to be very persistent. Although things are changing," she added thoughtfully. "Really they are. At least I like to hope they are. For women, I mean."

"Do you think we're actually going to get the vote?" I asked her. "I thought we surely would here in New Jersey, and then to be defeated so shamefully in October."

"Just a temporary setback," she said. "By 1920 we'll have it nationally. We already have it in several states, especially out west. Do you know Colorado once had a woman governor? Do you follow the suffrage movement? Do you have an active group here in Winter Hill?" I nodded my head but had no opportunity to say anything more as she rushed on. "I've never discussed this with my sister. The whole idea of women's rights makes her absolutely livid. All she wants me to do is get married. She keeps introducing me to one respectable red-faced burgher after another—all carbon copies of my sainted brother-in-law."

"She seems lots older than you," I ventured.

"Oh, she is," Sally said. "Twenty years. Really like another mother, I guess."

"Where did you go to college?" I asked.

"Bryn Mawr," she said. "That's where I first became active in the women's movement."

"Did you march in the big parade in New York a couple of months ago?" I asked. I was a bit shocked at the very idea.

"Sure," she said, nodding. "It was fun, actually. I was scared to death the first time I was at a rally. But after that it was easy. It's exciting."

"Are all the girls at college suffragettes?" I asked.

She hooted so loudly that for a moment the others in the room turned and looked at her quizzically. But then they turned back to their own conversations. I guess they were used to hoots from Sally Carruthers. "Of course not," she said. "There are all kinds of girls at college. All kinds."

"But not my kind," I said. "My parents would never let me go to college."

She looked me right in the eyes, the smile gone from her face. "What do you mean by your kind?" she asked.

I looked right back at her. "Jewish," I said firmly.

"Of course there are Jewish girls at college," Sally said. "At Bryn Mawr there were five or six Jewish girls just in my class."

"Mama thinks a Jewish girl can't go to college because there's nothing for her to eat there."

"Nothing to eat! What on earth do you mean?

There's plenty to eat. It may not exactly be home cooking, but you can survive on it."

"But it's not kosher," I explained. "We can only eat meat that's been killed a certain way. And we can't cook meat in the same pot that's been used for milk or eat it from the same dish."

"My lord, it sounds complicated," Sally said.

"It's really not hard at all," I said, ". . . after the first time."

Sally laughed. "Touché," she said. "Look, I can just tell you're a live one. If you want to go badly enough, you'll find a way. Now that I think about it, Etta Levy and Dolly Goldfarb commuted. They came to Bryn Mawr every day on the trolley. They lived in Philadelphia."

"I couldn't go to Philadelphia every day on the train from Winter Hill," I said. "It's much too long a trip."

"Bryn Mawr isn't the only school in the world," Sally said. "What about Barnard? That's in New York City. It's the girls' school of Columbia University. There're lots of Jewish girls there. I know it."

"Germans," I said. "They don't really count. A lot of them don't care what they eat. I guess I could learn not to care," I admitted suddenly. "But it would upset my mother too much. That is, if I could ever talk her into letting me go at all. Which I couldn't."

"Do you have a relative in New York?" she said. "Someone you could board with?"

Of course I did. I had never thought of that. Bubbie and Zadie. They lived on Delancey Street, on the Lower

East Side. Now that all their children were grown and gone, they complained that they rattled around in their flat like two peas in an empty pod. "I do," I said. "But it's all so unlikely. My parents . . ."

"I had a lot of talking to do too," Sally said. "It wasn't easy for me. I think the only reason I won was because my father got sick of hearing about it. He's always given me my way anyhow. If money's a problem, and you're very smart, maybe you can get a scholarship."

I shook my head. "I don't believe money's a problem." There was never loose money around our house. Mama had stern ideas about waste. But lately my father had been buying property. His lawyer, William Vanderbush, had come to our apartment once and he had joked with my father. He had said if this kept up, Papa would own all of Winter Hill in a couple of years. And Papa had just laughed back and answered, "All that you don't own, Mr. Vanderbush." There was always enough money for whatever Papa considered important. At least there had been within my memory. Mama explained that it had been different before we had come to Winter Hill, and the first few years afterward too. "Prosperity never lasts," she said. "You have to save for a rainy day." That was why she saw no reason to move into a house or buy an automobile or do anything extravagant like that. But there was no doubt about the fact that Papa had come a long way since he'd first arrived in Winter Hill fifteen years before and earned his living selling notions and fabrics to farmers from a pack he carried on his back.

"If you have money," Sally said, "I really don't think you're facing very serious difficulties at all."

"You don't know my parents," I said. "You just don't know them."

"Want to enough," Sally said, "and you will!"

I smiled. "I could always just eat vegetables," I said.

"That's it!" she agreed enthusiastically. "Now you've got the right idea."

Then I saw Peter coming toward us. "I've been looking all over for you!" he exclaimed. "Now that Aunt Sally's captured you, you'll never escape. She'll talk your ear off."

"You never told me about your Aunt Sally," I said. "I could listen to her all night." Warmth suffused me though, because he was there, and I smiled up at him.

"I bet," Peter said. "I didn't want you to know I had an aunt like her. She's the black sheep. You tend to have too many radical ideas as it is. Next thing I know, you'll be taking up socialism."

I thought of all my father's property and shook my head. "Not very likely," I replied.

"Come," he said, holding out his hand. "You've met my aunt; now I want you to meet my mother."

I had dreaded this moment. Talking to Sally, I'd pushed it out of my mind, but now it had to be faced.

"I'll see you later," Sally said gently. "After you've done your duty."

I held Peter's hand tightly. "Mama always likes to meet the people who've never been here before," he explained as he led me to the breakfast room where Mr. and Mrs. van Ruysdaal were seated, drinking coffee. "Mother, Father," he said, "I'd like you to meet Rebecca Levitsky, valedictorian of the senior class."

"Peter," I protested, "we don't know yet who the valedictorian will be. Probably you." I removed my hand hastily from his and dropped it to my side.

"My record is besmirched with one or two B's," Peter said. "I don't believe yours is."

"Oh, I know Rebecca," Mrs. van Ruysdaal said. "I've seen you often in your father's store, haven't I, Becky?"

"Yes, ma'am," I said.

"Are you having a busy Christmas season?" she asked.

"Oh, yes," I replied. "Papa put in a line of Singer sewing machines this year and they're selling very well."

"A sewing machine is an expensive Christmas present," Mr. van Ruysdaal said.

"But a useful one," I said. "I guess most of the people who buy it at Christmas would buy it anyway."

"The Jewish storekeepers do well at Christmas," Mrs. van Ruysdaal said with a little laugh. She was a slender, blond, pretty woman. "It's lucky for them Christmas exists."

"*All* the storekeepers do well at Christmas," I replied coolly. I didn't feel very cool. "Mr. LaPierre's ready-to-wear does about the best business in town, Papa says."

"Mr. LaPierre carries very high quality merchandise," Mrs. van Ruysdaal said.

"So does Levitsky's," I said, "or I'm sure you wouldn't buy there!"

Peter was growing increasingly uncomfortable at the trend of our conversation. "I think I'll put on the victrola now," he said. "Come on, Becky, we'll roll up the rug in the front parlor and we can all dance." He walked out of the breakfast room unceremoniously. Before I followed him, I said, "Good-bye. Thank you for letting me come. I'm sure I'll see you again—in the store."

I decided I would say good-bye to Peter and leave. But before I could tell him I was going, he said, "As soon as I get this victrola going, we'll dance." Well, I did want to dance with him. I had thought there might be dancing at the party and I had practiced the turkey trot and the tango with Annie. Irene Castle I wasn't, but I'd get by.

So I danced with Peter and I danced with Solly and I danced with Dick and then I danced with Peter again. We did the fox trot and he held me very close to him. By that time, I was having too much fun to even think of leaving. I did not encounter Mrs. van Ruysdaal for the rest of the evening. Perhaps she went to bed. But before I left, I sought out Sally. I didn't want to leave without saying good-bye to her. I found her seated on the sofa in the back parlor, surrounded by an admiring group of young men, with a few disconsolate looking girls on the fringes of the crowd. She was smoking a cigarette. Then I was sure Mrs. van Ruysdaal had gone to bed.

"Miss Carruthers . . ." I began.

"Sally, please," she said, getting up.

"Well, Sally, then," I went on, "I just wanted to thank you—you gave me such good advice."

"Advice? I didn't tell you anything of any practical value."

"Well, heart, then," I said. "New determination."

She leaned forward and kissed me on the cheek. "Good luck, darling," she said. "When you come to New York, look me up. Peter can give you my address, but if he forgets, you just call the *American*."

"I will," I promised. "Good-bye, and thanks again for everything."

Peter was waiting in the hall with my coat. Solly, Abe, and Lilly had already left, because Peter had told them that he would walk me home. I protested. "You can't leave your guests," I said.

"Most of the ones I invited are already gone," Peter said. "Melie can do the proper to the rest of 'em."

"It's far," I said. "A mile there, a mile back."

"I feel so good," Peter said, "I'll run all the way home singing 'God Rest Ye Merry, Gentlemen' at the top of my lungs. O'Hagan'll arrest me." O'Hagan was Winter Hill's most prominent policeman.

But going we were in no hurry. We walked slowly through the silent streets. My left hand was mittened, but not my right. He had taken the right mitten off and handed it to me solemnly and kept my hand clasped tightly in his all the way home.

I did not want to spoil the pleasantness of the evening, but I had at last to say what was on my mind.

"Your mother doesn't like me." I did not add I told you so, but I did say, "I'm surprised she let you invite me to the party."

"It's my party," Peter said. "I invite whom I please. I'm not afraid of my mother."

"I'm not afraid of mine either," I said. "But I don't like to do things that'll upset her."

"My mother needs a little upsetting," Peter said with a bitterness I had not expected. "She thinks she knows everything. She won't let a fellow be. No matter how much you do, it's never enough for her. If I'm not valedictorian, she'll sulk for weeks."

"Oh, Peter . . ." I began.

"It's true," he said. "She won't say anything. She'll just walk around kind of hurt, like I was caught robbing a bank or something. I want her to know I'm my own person. I don't have to do what she wants me to do all the time just because she wants me to do it."

"So you invited me to the party." We were at our back steps now. I had pulled my hand out of his and put my mitten back on. "And you eat lunch with me every day in the back of Mr. Allison's room!"

"Do you think I do that to spite my mother?" Peter exclaimed. "My God, Becky, I had no idea you had such a low opinion of me. How can you even think such a thing?"

"What other reason can there be? Really, Peter," I went on. "When you look at it all objectively, what other reason can there be?"

"Oh, Becky," he cried, putting his arms around me. "It's yourself you have such a low opinion of, isn't it?

You're beautiful Becky, and I like you." He paused for a moment. "I love you," he whispered. Then he pulled me close to him and kissed me on the lips.

That kiss was delicious, warm and delicious, not at all like the damp exchanges I had experienced in games of Post Office and Spin the Bottle with Abe and Solly when I was in eighth grade. I hadn't been kissed since. Peter's was my first real one, and I kissed him back. I wasn't sure if I was supposed to, but I did anyway, because I wanted to. "Thank you, Peter," I said softly. I laughed a little. "Everything considered, it's been a wonderful evening."

"Good night, Becky," he said. "I'll come by to-morrow."

"No, no," I said hastily. "Don't do that. Please, Peter, not yet. You're braver than I am. I'm not ready for that yet."

"Well, I can't wait until school opens again to see you," he said, obviously annoyed. "That won't be for another week. I said I loved you, Becky. Don't you love me?"

"I—I don't know, Peter," I replied honestly. "I like you an awful lot, but I don't know much about love. . . . Dick said a whole bunch were going to the Bijou to-morrow to see the vaudeville. I'll meet you there if you'd like." The Bijou had vaudeville every Monday and Thursday, along with its regular motion picture bill.

"I guess that'll have to do," he said grudgingly. "For now. But if we're really going to go together, we can't do it in secret. I don't care what my mother or your mother says, I'm not going to sneak around."

"Tomorrow," I said. "I'll talk to you about it tomorrow. I can't think now, I really can't. With you standing right here, I can't think."

That seemed to restore his good humor. He kissed me again. Actually he kissed me again five or six times. "Good night, Becky," he said at last.

"Good night, Peter." And then I ran up the stairs as fast as my feet would carry me. The flat was silent; no one had waited up for me, thank goodness. I felt as if Peter's kisses must be visible all over my face. I got into bed as quickly as I could. Ruthie barely stirred, but it was a long time before I fell asleep.

Purim

"IF WE'RE REALLY going to go together, we can't do it in secret. I don't care what my mother or your mother says, I'm not going to sneak around." Peter said that to me the night of his party, and he said it to me at least a hundred other times in the months that followed.

Nothing he said, though, would persuade me to allow him to come to my house. "If my mother finds out," I said, "it's the end. That's all, the absolute and complete end. If you want to see me at all, it has to be this way."

"This way" was meeting at the library, sitting at the same table and trying to whisper under Miss Stragan's watchful eye. Or drinking root beer at the Candy Kitchen with a whole gang of other kids, while Peter rested his arm casually around the back of my chair, never actually touching me, for fear of giving the owner, Mr. Lerkey, something to talk about if he happened to run into my father or mother. Or eating our lunch, as we had now for several months, in the back of Mr. Allison's classroom, though we couldn't touch each other there either, not with Mr. Allison sometimes sitting at his own desk eating his own lunch, or returning to the room unexpectedly if he ate with another teacher.

It was winter, and cold, or else we could have met in the woods or fields that surrounded Winter Hill, which was in those days a country town. As it was, the only place we had any privacy at all was at the Bijou or the Regency. We'd meet there sometimes on Sunday afternoon. I always made sure to arrive after

Peter had already gone inside and I always paid my own nickel admission. Sometimes, for a special long movie, like *Birth of a Nation*, I had to pay a dime.

We sat in the very last row, and if it was a good picture, we watched it, but if we didn't care much about it, we did a lot of kissing and touching there in the dark. If it weren't for those spooning sessions at the pictures, I think Peter would have gotten sick of the whole business a lot sooner than he did. In all those weeks that he kept insisting that I let him call for me at my house, he never once suggested that I come to his. "I don't care what my mother or your mother says." But he cared, at least about what *his* mother said.

Sometimes I went to the pictures twice in one weekend—Sunday afternoon with Peter and Saturday night with Henry Braude. Luckily, they changed the bill every day. I must have gone out with Henry five or six times in the three months between Chanukah and Purim, to the pictures, or to a social at Allemand Hall. I didn't object too much when my mother suggested these outings. I considered them excellent diversionary tactics.

One night when Henry brought me home I even let him kiss me to see if it was anything like when Peter kissed me. It wasn't, so I didn't let him kiss me again. This didn't bother Henry. He attributed it to proper maidenly reserve, and assumed that I had permitted him to kiss me at all in a momentary lapse which my modesty later regretted. It's a good thing he never got a glimpse of Peter and me in the back of the Bijou. But Henry was so busy talking he never seemed to care if I was really listening. If I kept quiet and just mur-

mured "yes" now and then he appeared very well satisfied with my company. He never seemed to guess what I was thinking, or care. On the other hand, now that I look back on it, I realize the reverse was also true. He could not have been any more self-centered than I.

March came. Instead of snow, we had rain now, but for Purim, there was still no real spring. Annie wanted to go with us to the *megillah* reading. She didn't want to go with her in-laws. Sid still wasn't home. He had discovered that his aunt had passed away in a charity hospital but now he was having difficulty settling her estate. Her husband's family wanted her house, but they didn't want to pay for it. I think that in Annie's mind Sid had become a remote figure, like someone who had died. She had mourned him, but now she was forgetting him.

And yet he wrote. He wrote every week. He said that things were coming to a head, that surely he would be able to start for home soon. But he had written that before. Deep down inside, she didn't really believe him.

Actually, Mr. and Mrs. Klein were glad to get out of the *megillah* reading. They had only been going for Annie's sake, and when she said I had asked her to accompany our family, they were happy to be spared the noise and confusion of the Purim celebration. Mrs. Klein was famous for her *hammentashen*, the three-cornered pastries stuffed with prune, apricot, or poppy seed, which were traditional for the holiday, and she had made enough of them to feed every Jew in town after services. She had done her bit and could stay home with impunity. Mrs. Klein was a Puritan, and she did not enjoy the gaiety that prevailed after the *megillah* reading, when some of the men drank a good deal of whiskey and sweet red wine. Tradition said that on Purim—and on Purim only—it was permissible to drink until one could not tell Mordecai from Haman.

The *shamos*, Mr. Gordon, stood in the doorway of Allemand Hall when we got there and handed out noisemakers to all who wanted them. Everyone under twenty-five took one, and that included Annie, Ruth, and me. The rabbi chanted the *megillah*, the Biblical book of Esther, and every time he mentioned the name of the villainous Haman who tried to kill all the Jews, we whirled our noisemakers furiously. And even the youngest among us knew that every time he whirled that *gragger*, every time he shouted and stamped his feet at the mention of the name Haman, he was symbolically destroying all the enemies who had made Jews suffer since their days in Egypt—Romans, generals, Spanish inquisitors, and the warring Russian and Austrian soldiers of our own day.

No one whirled her noisemaker harder or stamped her feet louder or shouted more enthusiastically than Annie. In some ways she seemed younger than Ruth. Ruth was Queen Esther in the Purim play the Hebrew school students put on after services. Her red braids were piled on her head and she wore a beautiful green dress with an enormous hoop skirt that she and her friend Carrie Kyle had found in a trunk in Carrie's attic. I had been so preoccupied all year I hadn't noticed until that very moment how tall she had gotten, and how beautiful. She played her part with such sweetness and dignity that I could not believe this was Ruthie, my spoiled, smart-alecky baby sister. I had a sudden oppressive feeling that time was getting away from me, flying by faster than I wanted it to. It was March. In three months I would graduate and still nothing was settled. I had not discussed going to Barnard with Mama and Papa. I feared mentioning college to them as much as I feared their finding out about Peter.

I was supposed to go to the pictures with Henry the Saturday night after Purim, but I had to call him up on the telephone in the store to break our appointment. I told him Ruth didn't feel well and I had to stay with her because Mama and Papa were going to play cards with Mr. and Mrs. Gordon. He wanted to come over and sit with me, but I said no, what Ruth had might be catching. Mama and Papa were at the Gordons', all right, but Ruth had gone with them. I didn't want to tell Henry the real reason I broke our date, which was that Annie Klein was sobbing her eyes out in our parlor and Sid Klein was staring at her disconsolately and shaking his head, when he wasn't shouting. Henry would find out about Annie soon enough; he didn't have to hear it from me.

Sid had come home that day. He had come home unexpectedly. For some unaccountable reason he had decided to surprise both his parents and Annie. Perhaps he had not wanted to write that he was about to sail for fear some other unexpected event would delay him once again, and once again disappoint Annie. So he had just taken the train home from New York after his ship had docked, and walked into his apartment about three o'clock in the afternoon shouting, "Surprise." What had never occurred to him during all that long journey, as he had savored the look that he imagined would come over Annie's face when first she saw him, was that she wouldn't be home. Knowing Annie as he did, it was not very realistic of him to imagine that she would be sitting in her parlor or her kitchen all those weary months he was gone, just waiting for him.

Well, as he told us afterward, he was disappointed when he arrived and found the flat empty, but he realized that he had been foolish to imagine that she would be there in the middle of a Saturday afternoon, and so he went down to the store to greet his parents and find out where Annie was. They, of course, were thrilled and surprised to see him, and there was much hugging and kissing and talking all at once before he could ask about Annie, but finally his father told him that she had taken the train and gone to Newark to visit her father and little brothers and sisters for the day. She had said she would be back about seven or eight o'clock in the evening.

Sid had expressed his disapproval of Annie's coming home alone after dark. His mother had assured him acidly that once Annie made up her mind to something there really was no stopping her. Sid resolved to meet every train that came in from six on. There were only a few on a Saturday evening; it wasn't a very difficult thing to do. He walked back home between trains and ate his supper at his mother's house.

Annie was on the 8:42. But she wasn't alone. A young man helped her off the train. That in itself was nothing. But, unaccountably, he held her arm tightly as they walked down the platform. They were so busy laughing and talking and looking into each other's eyes that they did not see Sid, waiting at the top of the steps.

Annie had not gone to visit her father. She had gone into New York with Mr. Allison. They had gone to the vaudeville at the Palace. Then they had had supper at Downey's. It had been nothing but the most innocent pleasure, as Annie later kept telling Sid over and over again. Perhaps it had been a mistake, but it had been an unmeaning one, committed out of loneliness and boredom. Annie and Mr. Allison and Sid had finally encountered each other at the end of the station platform.

"That meeting," I said to Annie hours and hours later when we were talking about it, "that meeting must have been the worst moment of your life."

"No, it wasn't," Annie said. "Not at first. At first I was so surprised to see Sid I couldn't think of anything else. It was only a minute or two later, when I realized he hadn't kissed me, when I looked in his face, that I knew something terrible had happened. And then I introduced him to Ken, and Ken held out his hand, and Sid wouldn't take it. And then Ken said I should have let him get off the train at Brookville, like he had suggested. That was the very worst thing he could have mentioned. I got mad and said there wasn't anything wrong in two acquaintances riding on a train together. But that of course made Sid even more suspicious than he was before and it all came out—all about Downey's, and the vaudeville, and everything. But so what? I had never meant it to be a secret. There wasn't anything wrong with it. Only to Mama Klein." When she said "Mama" she made it sound like a curse word.

But that wasn't really true, and Annie knew it. The whole town had thought there was something going on between Annie and Mr. Allison. Mrs. Klein wasn't the only one. And now Sid thought so too. He didn't say anything to Annie in front of Mr. Allison. Perhaps he was too shocked to say anything. But it was a far different homecoming from the one he imagined—or the one Annie had imagined, before she had stopped imagining it. And the argument between them, after they had gotten home, grew hotter and hotter, with Mrs. Klein's malignant presence serving to fan the flames.

Maybe Sid would have been more understanding if his mother hadn't been there to tell him all about the meetings between Annie and Mr. Allison in Cartland's Pharmacy.

Finally Annie had not been able to stand it anymore. She had flown out of her house and down the three blocks to ours, with Sid after her all the way. Fortunately for all concerned, Mrs. Klein's bulk was too great to permit her to join the pursuit.

And so Annie sat in our parlor, trying, between sobs, to explain herself to Sid. But no matter what she said, it was the wrong thing. He could not understand. She had been lonely. So had he, he said. There was no one to talk with except his mother, who didn't like her. He had had no one to talk to either. In Warsaw he had all kinds of opportunities to do things that men were expected to do when they were away from home, but he hadn't done them. He had remained faithful, and it was harder for him than for her. Why hadn't she?

Annie's anger triumphed over her misery and guilt. "What makes you think I was unfaithful?" she asked. "How come you don't trust me at all? You trust your mother, not me. All I did was talk to Mr. Allison— that's absolutely all. And yet you believe all the lies your mother's poisoned your mind with, not what I say! You think it was easier for me than it was for you, all those months you were gone? Why do you think that? It isn't any easier for a woman than a man. It isn't. If you believe it is, it shows that you don't understand me, and you never did!"

"Understand?" Sid shouted. "Understand? What's to understand? I don't know how far you went with this Mr. Allison, and I don't care. Carrying on with him in front of the whole town is enough for me."

Annie began to sob again, more quietly now. I could not help putting my arm around her heaving shoulders. Sid shot me a dirty look. Maybe he thought I was in cahoots with Annie. "Let's go home now, Annie," he said in a quieter voice. "Let's go home and talk things over together. We can't go on dragging Becky into our troubles. She's too young to involve in all of this."

But Annie wouldn't go home with him. No matter what he said, she refused to return to his house. Finally, my parents came home, with Ruth. Annie and Sid sat silently, while in whispers in the kitchen I told Mama and Papa what had happened. My mother gently joined her entreaties to Sid's. I think she feared that if Annie stayed away one night, it would be easier for her to stay away a second and a third and a fourth and so on forever. But Annie would not be moved, and at last Sid left. She and I talked for a long time. Or rather she talked to me, going over the same ground again and again. She cried a lot and then, at last, she dozed off for a bit on our sofa.

In the morning, crumpled and bleary-eyed, she rose and asked me to accompany her back to her house. Only she did not call it her house. She called it Mama Klein's house, saying "Mama" in that same derisive way. Sid was there when we arrived, but she did not speak to him. She did not say one word to him, though he followed her all over the flat, scolding her. Perhaps if he had said one kind or tender word, she might have relented, but he was so bitter at the wrong he felt he had suffered, that he could not speak to her in a reasonable way.

She washed her face and hands and changed her dress. She removed two cardboard suitcases from the storeroom in back of her apartment and quickly filled them with clothes. I knew now why she had insisted I come with her. With me present, it was not possible for Sid to forcibly restrain her. If my mother had known she was going to ask me to come, she probably would not have let me, but we had left our house before my parents or Ruthie had awakened.

Together, we walked out of Sid's house. This time Sid did not follow. He let her go. I went with her to the station, carrying one of her bags. We said very little. She told me only that she was going back to her father's in Newark. She promised to get in touch with me when she was settled and let me know what was happening. I kissed her when we got to the waiting room where she had to buy her ticket, but I did not wait with her. I went back home.

I was so confused. I didn't know what to think. My parents were awake by the time I got home. I sat with them at the kitchen table, drinking coffee and trying to straighten out what had happened.

"I felt so sorry for Annie," I said. "I wanted to cry when I left her there in that station, all alone."

"It's Sid you should feel sorry for," Papa said. "She did a terrible thing."

"He never should have left her. I said from the beginning it was a mistake for him to go," Mama said.

"That's no excuse," Papa said. "Other women have been left and have not behaved like that. Your own mother stayed behind in Europe while your father went on ahead. She was alone for two years and she didn't do what Annie did."

"But what did Annie do?" I asked. "In actuality, what did she do?"

"You're too young to understand," Mama said.

"Oh, come on, Mama," I said. "You don't really believe that. I've read too much and heard too much

not to have some idea of what goes on in this world."
I thought of Peter and what we might have liked to do together if we had dared, and I blushed. "Anyway," I went on hastily, "I don't believe that Annie actually did anything bad. Do you?"

Mama shook her head. "I don't know. If only she had had a baby." She turned to Papa. "My mother had babies."

"She could have helped in the store," Papa said.

"Oh, Papa," I cried angrily, "you know Mrs. Klein wouldn't let her cross the threshold of that precious store."

"Perhaps she could have done something else," Papa suggested.

"What?" I asked. "Here in Winter Hill, what? Married women don't work unless they're poor Irish or Italian or Polish immigrants who scrub someone's floor or do piece work in the lace factory. What was Annie fit to do? What had she ever expected to do, except get married? That's a mistake, Papa. Don't you see now that that's a mistake? I've learned my lesson," I announced firmly. "I'm not marrying any man until I'm just as good as he is."

"But of course you're just as good as any man," Mama said. "You come from a good family, you're intelligent, you're pretty, you can keep a kosher home, you're not poor . . ."

"Oh, Mama," I insisted, "that's not what I mean. I don't mean a list of attributes. I have to be me, a person."

"Don't you think Mama's a person?" Papa said.

"Of course, of course she is," I cried. "But I have to get to be one in my own way."

"Is that what Annie was doing?" Papa asked sarcastically. "Becoming a person? Better she should have stayed a nobody."

I tried to stay calm. "Look," I explained reasonably, "I'm not saying she did the right thing. I know what she did was terrible. But it wasn't all her fault. You can't treat a person like a child all her life, and then all of a sudden expect her to act grown-up. A woman isn't a child," I went on. "She's a whole person, just like a man. Or she ought to be, anyway. You have a wife and two daughters, Papa. You ought to know that."

"I thought I did," Papa replied mildly.

"Do you, Papa? Do you really? Well, I'll tell you something, Papa. I've decided what I want to do after I graduate. I want to go to college."

"*Oy vey*," Mama muttered. "Our Rifka is going out of her mind. This whole business has made her crazy."

"Really, Molly," Papa said, "I don't see what Annie has to do with Rebecca's wanting to go to college."

"Everything, Papa," I said, shaking my head slowly. "Everything. Can't you see that? I'm going to study Greek and Latin and Hebrew and maybe be a professor one day. In a college. I'll even publish books."

"Don't be ridiculous," Papa replied flatly.

"If I were your son," I retorted, "you'd let me go to college. You'd *want* me to go to college. If I were your son, you wouldn't be content for me to work in the store. You'd want me to be a lawyer or a doctor or something."

"You're not my son," Papa said. "You're my daughter. And what I want for you is a husband and a home and a family." He spoke with perfect calmness. Papa was not a yeller. He left emotionalism to Mama and to me.

But I wasn't calm anymore. I found myself shouting at him. "But what about me? What about what I want?"

"Rifka, shut up," Mama yelled. "How dare you raise your voice to Papa?"

Papa gave Mama a look so quelling that she stopped talking. He didn't need Mama to protect him from his own children. Then he said to me, "I will not discuss anything with you when you are in such a state. Go to your room. We will talk about it later when you have calmed down."

But we didn't talk about it later. I tried to bring it up again at dinner, but he said we were not to ruin dinner with foolish conversations. I could not understand him. Though in the end we always did what Papa wanted in our house, it was not like him to behave in an unreasonable manner. He always talked about things with us; he always told us why he wanted us to do or not do a certain thing.

Between Annie's tragic departure and my father's refusal to even discuss college, I was so miserable the next day that everything Peter said put me on edge.

We were eating our lunch, as usual, in the back of

Mr. Allison's classroom. Mr. Allison was eating his at his desk while he read his newspaper. I found it ironic that the incident which had absolutely ruined Annie's life hadn't affected his at all.

"Mabel's having a party Saturday night," Peter said.

"I know," I replied. "A taffy pull."

"I want to take you," he said.

"Of course. I'll be there." I liked parties. Then Peter and I could be together without difficulty. But I didn't get invited to very many.

"That's not what I mean," Peter went on. "I don't want to meet you there. I want to take you there. I want to come for you at your house and take you there."

"Oh, Peter," I said wearily. "We've been through all that a thousand times. I will not go out with you openly. I will not do that to my parents."

"Well, I am sick," he said loudly, "sick to death of going out with you secretly." Mr. Allison looked up from his newspaper. I think the glance he shot us was sympathetic.

"Sh," I whispered. "He'll hear you. It's not exactly secret. Everyone in Winter Hill High knows all about it."

He nodded. "Exactly," he whispered back. "So how much longer can we keep it from your mother?"

He was right. I was sick of the whole business too. I was sick of everything. All of the terrible things we said to each other in the next few moments we had to say in whispers so low we could hardly hear each other. That made the whole conversation even more frightful. It made me feel as if I were at the bottom of a pit, and snow was falling on top of me and burying me so that no matter how loud I screamed, no one could hear me.

"I cannot openly defy my parents," I whispered. "I cannot do that. Especially at this time. Besides, as long as they don't know I'm seeing you, they can't forbid me to do it."

"Then you don't love me," Peter said.

"That's right, Peter," I said seriously. "I don't know if I love you. But I do know that I love them."

"You've got to grow up, Becky," Peter said. "They can't go on being the most important people in your life forever. You're afraid of them!"

"Well, I guess that's part of it," I admitted. "Do you know, if I married a boy who wasn't Jewish, my mother would mourn me as if I were dead?"

"No one's talking about getting married," Peter interjected hastily.

"Of course not," I agreed. "I'm just trying to give you an idea of how they feel."

"They're so medieval. How can anyone have ideas like that in the twentieth century?"

I did not like Peter speaking against my parents. I despaired of ever making him understand. "Peter," I said, "you can't comprehend what they've been through. That's what makes them the way they are. And my problem is that I'm not sure they're wrong. That's why I have to go along with them. At least for now, until I've worked it all out in my own mind."

"It's perfectly clear to me that you don't feel the

same about me as I do about you." His face wore its petulant expression, the expression that only people who knew Peter van Ruysdaal really well ever saw. I knew where I'd seen it before. On his mother's face. "I think you've been leading me on, Becky."

"Oh, Peter," I cried—softly—"I like you. I like you so much. This has nothing to do with you. This is killing me. Don't you know that? It's killing me."

Peter did not believe that. "You should have the courage of your convictions, Becky."

"But Peter," I agonized, "I don't know what my convictions are!"

"At seventeen you ought to, Becky. You're an American. And so am I. That's what should come first."

"I can't defy the people I love best," I said. "Not yet, anyway. I wish everything was as clear to me as it is to you."

"Some new female you are!" he muttered furiously. "My Aunt Sally wouldn't behave like this."

That was hitting below the belt. He knew how much I admired his Aunt Sally. "Your Aunt Sally has nothing to do with this," I said angrily. "This is between you and me."

"And your mother and your father," he screamed, sotto voce.

"And your mother too," I answered. "Don't forget that."

"You still think I liked you to spite her." I noticed he used the past tense.

"You brought that up again," I said. "Not me."

"Anyone who can think that not only doesn't love

me—she doesn't even like me," he whispered indignantly. "I should have known. You're narrow, you're clannish, you're anti-social—just like all the other . . ." Suddenly he realized what he was going to say, and closed his mouth.

"Go ahead," I said. "Say it. Say it. Just like all the other Jews. I knew that was how you felt. I knew that was how you felt all the time."

A terribly sad look came over his face. He shook his head silently and got to his feet. Without saying goodbye, he walked out of the classroom.

I sat there for a long time. I had done it to him. I had driven him to say something I knew the best part of him really didn't mean. And he had driven me to say things the best part of me didn't mean. I felt sick, absolutely sick, to my stomach. When I'm emotionally upset, I always feel like vomiting.

Finally I stood up. I told Mr. Allison that I felt terrible and that I didn't think I'd stay for afternoon classes. He looked at me as if he wanted to say something, but he didn't. He only nodded.

I walked home. When I got there, I told Mama I was sick because I had my period, and I locked myself in the bathroom. There was no other place in our flat where privacy was possible. I sat crouched on the toilet most of the afternoon. The others had to use the bathroom in the back of the store. When they asked me through the door what was the matter, I told them I had bad cramps. And there, finally, I let myself cry. I cried and cried and cried until at last there were no tears left.

Passover

PETER VAN RUYSDAAL didn't say one word to me for the next month, unless he had to talk to me about the annual at a meeting. I was completely miserable. Maybe, I thought, maybe I was in love with Peter van Ruysdaal. After all, how did I know what love was? If it wasn't feeling absolutely marvelous when someone kissed you, then what was it? And if it wasn't feeling like dirt when someone ignored you, then what was it?

But if Peter had loved me, as he had said he did, he would not now treat me as if I had the smallpox, making no attempt at all to understand the things I had been trying to explain to him. He had thought I didn't love him. Now it seemed to me maybe I did, only he hadn't really loved me. The situation was ironic, but I was certainly not able to laugh at it.

Peter started going around again with Isabel Liebig, and with a vengeance. I found their behavior disgusting. He was always grabbing her in the cloakroom, and they didn't seem to care who saw them. For the first time in his life, Dick Evans was really mad at Peter. When Peter had been occupied with me, Dick had had Isabel all to himself. But all Peter had had to do was crook his finger and Isabel had come running, dropping Dick like a can of worms.

One day when I came into the cloakroom to get my things, I saw Isabel quickly throw her arms around Peter's neck. I suddenly realized that she was performing for my benefit, and perhaps he was too. It certainly seemed to me that he glanced at me before he bent to kiss her. Perhaps the pangs of unrequited love were disturbing me—but so were the pangs of plain old unromantic jealousy.

At least I was sure now that if he didn't love me, he didn't love Isabel Liebig either. No one would put on a public performance in a cloakroom with a girl he loved. If a man really loved a woman, he respected her too. At least that's what was said in all the movies I'd watched at the Bijou and the Regency.

Anyway, I was tired to death of mooning around like a sick cat, feeling as if I were going to throw up every other minute. It was time to act. Maybe all that stuff about respect that I'd seen in the movies was true, and maybe it wasn't, but there were a few things I was sure of. I'd learned more in the back row of the Bijou than what was taking place on the screen. I had learned something about Peter van Ruysdaal's effect on me, but I'd learned something about my effect on him too. I was willing to lay dollars to doughnuts that he could hug and kiss Isabel Liebig from now until tomorrow and walk out of the cloakroom or the Bijou or wherever it was without so much as a drop of sweat on his high, fine forehead. I could show that Isabel Liebig a thing or two and, I decided, it was about time I did!

We had a party in Mr. Allison's room after we finally put the annual to bed. Mr. Allison explained that "put to bed" was newspaper talk for "hand over to the printer." Mr. Allison had pretty well recovered from the episode with Annie. After all, nothing had happened to him because of it. I was the only one of his students who even knew about it, and I, of course, wasn't talking. He was saved by the fact that he had been involved with a Jewish woman. All the Jews of Winter Hill knew what had happened, but they were no more about to tell anyone else than I was.

I had brought oatmeal cookies for the party, Mabel had brought hermits, and Isabel had brought several large jars filled with pink lemonade. But after we ate the cookies and drank the lemonade and congratulated each other on having pulled the whole thing off, there was little left to do or say. A party at school was not like a party at someone's house. At least it hadn't been since fourth grade when your mother sent cupcakes if it was your birthday, and your teacher made you a paper crown.

Peter was the first to call it quits. He said his mother hadn't been feeling well lately, and she really got nervous if he was too late, so he'd better get on home. He told Isabel to stay for the rest of the party and that he'd see her later. I knew everyone else would leave soon after Peter did, so I grabbed a couple of the empty lemonade jars and said I'd wash them out in the girls' room. I left quickly so none of the others could offer to come along to help me.

I ran as fast as I could down the hall to Miss Krieter's room. Sure enough, Peter was still there getting his coat. I had made up my mind what I was going to do, and though my heart was in my throat, I went through with it. "Peter," I said to him, "wait a minute." My voice was louder than usual because I had been afraid that I wouldn't be able to get anything out at all.

"Yes?" Peter asked flatly. "What do you want?"

"Look, Peter," I said. "This is ridiculous. Just because we can't go together doesn't mean we have to be enemies."

"We're not enemies," Peter replied. "What makes you think we're enemies?"

"You do, Peter. Because you won't speak to me."

"That's not true."

"You speak to me only when you have to. You never *say* anything to me. We used to have a lot to say to each other."

"It was different then."

"We were friends, Peter. And you asked me if you could come to my house for Passover, and I said I'd try to arrange it. Well, come, Peter. Come for Seder, our big Passover dinner."

"Why should I?" he asked sullenly.

I was growing discouraged, but I persisted. "Because then maybe you'll understand a little bit. Being Jewish is so complicated, Peter. If you come to our house for Seder, then maybe you'll start to understand." I meant what I said. It wasn't the only reason for asking him, but it was a real one. I was no saint, and even a saint's motives aren't always pure. "I'm going to ask Mabel and Dick to come too, if you'll come," I added.

He was silent for a moment as he looked at me thoughtfully. His curiosity or his better nature won the debate he was carrying on inside of himself. "O.K.," he said with a small smile. "I'll come, if the others can come. When is it?"

"April seventeenth," I said. "Six o'clock. That's

swell. That's really swell. I'll speak to the others to-morrow." I smiled back at him. I was really so excited that I forgot about the jars I was supposed to wash and left them sitting on a desk in Miss Krieter's room. I was in a hurry to get home. I had a problem. I had not yet told my mother that I wanted Peter, Dick, and Mabel to come for Seder. Dick and Mabel were just cover for Peter so I had decided that there was no point in fighting the whole thing out with her unless I was sure Peter would come, because if I got her permission and then he didn't come, she would regard that as further proof of the inimical anti-semitism she saw everywhere anyway. But now it occurred to me that if I could not persuade my mother to let Peter come, and had to withdraw the invitation, Peter would be further confirmed in his picture of Jews as clannish and un-friendly. I hadn't thought of that before.

All the way up the stairs I could smell the cabbage soup my mother was cooking for supper. It smelled marvelous. Mama was a superb cook. With supper safely bubbling away on the stove, she was ironing when I came into the kitchen.

"Bring me the hot iron," she said as soon as she saw me, "and put this one back on the stove." Papa had not yet been able to persuade Mama that an electric iron would not burn all our clothes to a crisp.

I switched the irons for her. "My goodness, the soup smells wonderful," I said.

"Tell Ruthie," Mama replied. "She hates cabbage soup."

"What does she know? She doesn't like *gefilte* fish

either. I can't wait for Passover. *Gefilte* fish. *Matzoh* balls. *Taiglach*. You're such a wonderful cook, Mama. You should really write a book."

"Don't be silly," she replied. But she smiled. "I wouldn't know what to put down. I never measure anything."

"I wish some of my friends from school could taste your cooking," I said casually. "It would be an education for them."

"Oh, they wouldn't like it," Mama said. "They just like ham and sausage and things like that."

"Oh, Mama, don't be silly. They would be very interested to taste your cooking. And they'd like to find out more about our religion too. I think you should let me have some of them over for Seder."

"Strangers? For Seder?" Mama shook her head. "Oh, no, Becky, I don't think that's a good idea at all. In Russia there was always trouble around Pesach."

"Mama, my friends don't think we make *matzohs* out of blood. No one thinks that in the United States. You ought to let them come, so they could really find out something about our religion. You know it says right in the *Haggadah*, 'Let all who are hungry enter and eat.'"

That impressed her. "I'll discuss it with your father," she said.

I was pleased. She was no longer saying no.

At supper I brought the idea up again. I couldn't wait for her to discuss it with Papa on her own. I had to know by the next day.

"Who did you want to have?" Papa asked.

"Oh, Mabel and Dick and Peter," I said. "We've gotten so friendly, you know, because of the annual. I know all about their religion. A Jew can't help knowing a lot about Christianity, just from going to school. But they don't know anything about my religion, and I think they should. I think you should let them come to the Seder."

"You know, Molly," Papa said to Mama, "it's not a bad idea. This morning, after the *minyan*, I was talking with Jake Baumgartner and Sam Polansky." Early each morning, before he opened the store, Papa went to Allemand Hall where he joined several other observant men in reciting the morning prayers. "Sam said that the synagogue will be done in a few months, and we should have a parade when we dedicate it."

"A parade?" Ruthie asked. "With drums and horns, like on the Fourth of July?"

Papa laughed. "Not quite, honey," he said. "More like we have on Simchas Torah, when we take the scrolls out of the ark and march them around the sanctuary. The parade would be for moving the scrolls of the law from Allemand Hall to the new synagogue. All the men and boys would take turns carrying the scrolls in the front, and everyone else would follow behind. Every Jew in town would be in the parade. We'd march straight down Main Street from Allemand Hall to B'nai Avraham." That was the name of our new congregation—Sons of Abraham—because that had been the name of the burial society which had gotten the building started.

"The town would never let us," Mama said. "And

even if they did, all the people would come out and stare at us. Some of them might start to throw things. I don't think it's a good idea at all."

"That's what Jake said," Papa said. "But I don't agree. I like Sam's idea."

"It would be better just to put the scrolls in Jake Baumgartner's Packard and drive them over," Mama said.

"But the Talmud says the scrolls should be carried, the way the ark of the covenant was carried through the wilderness for forty years."

Mama had no answer to that. She believed, even more strongly than Papa, in doing what the Talmud said to do.

I moved in quickly. "If we're going to have a parade, we'd better start getting people used to some of our ways," I remarked, sounding like sweet reason itself.

Papa nodded thoughtfully. "Yes," he said. "Let Becky's friends come, Molly. Let them taste your cooking. We always have such a crowd, three more won't make any difference. They did invite Becky at Christmas. It's only polite to return the favor."

Mama shook her head. "They're going to think we're a bunch of barbarians."

"Mama," I said, "sometimes I think you're ashamed to be Jewish."

My mother turned on me angrily. "I am proud to be Jewish!" she said. "Too proud to want to be laughed at behind my back!"

"They'll understand," I said. "People who understand won't laugh. I'll make them understand."

"I plan to live in this town until I die," Papa said. "It's a good town; I hope my children will live here after me. So it's time the town started to learn who we are."

"Our grandparents thought we were going to live in the *shtetl* in Russia forever too," Mama said.

"Let them come," Papa said. "Let them come." When Papa wanted it, he had the last word.

Henry Braude came for Pesach too, but not Aunt Rachel and Uncle Moishe. They had gone to Brooklyn to spend the holiday with Aunt Rachel's brother. Their places were filled by Bubbie and Zadie Isaacs from New York, who had come to stay with us. I liked my broad-faced, babushkaed grandmother and my frail, gentle grandfather, though we literally did not speak the same language. They spoke to me in Yiddish, I spoke to them in English. We managed to understand each other.

When Mabel, Dick, and Peter arrived, I introduced them to Bubbie and Zadie. Bubbie could tell right away they weren't Jewish. I knew that from the way she lifted her eyebrows. But Zadie was ever the gentleman and scholar, and fortunately it was he who was moderately fluent in English, not Bubbie. He shook hands and said, "How do you do? Permit me to offer the greetings of the season."

"How do you do, sir?" Peter said. "A very happy holiday to you, too."

"We're really happy that Becky invited us," Mabel said. "We know it's going to be awfully interesting."

She giggled nervously. "Once I went to a Catholic mass."

My grandfather looked rather puzzled, but he smiled a little smile and nodded.

"Dummy," Dick said, poking her in the ribs. "You're the only girl I know stupid enough to mix up Jews and Catholics. What does a Jewish Passover have to do with a mass?"

More than you'll ever know, I thought to myself. Obviously no one had ever told Dick that the Last Supper was a Passover Seder, or that the body and blood Jesus had held up before his disciples were a *matzoh* cracker and a glass of ritual wine. Well, I wasn't going to go into all of that now. "Come on," I said. "I'll show you where you're supposed to sit." I led them to the far end of the long table which stretched from the kitchen through the parlor. We couldn't have one table set in the parlor and another in the kitchen for Pesach. We all had to be at the same table because the meal on the first two nights of Passover is actually a lengthy service called the Seder in which all must participate.

I put Mabel next to Henry Braude, and I sat opposite, with Dick and Peter on either side.

"You'll have to explain things to Mabel," I said to Henry.

"Oh would you, please?" Mabel said, smiling up at him, and actually batting her lashes. It had never occurred to me that someone might find Henry attractive, but when I made myself look at him as Mabel probably did, I saw a tall, slender, but well-built man, with black, curly hair. Even with his glasses, there was a mephistophelian handsomeness about his large, heavy-lidded brown eyes.

"I'd be delighted," Henry said, smiling. He pulled out Mabel's chair and seated her gracefully. They were set for the evening. I introduced Dick to my cousin Fanny who was seated on his left. She was only fourteen, but "advanced for her age." That was the polite way of putting it.

"My friend Dick isn't Jewish," I said to Fanny. "You'll have to explain things to him."

"Not Jewish?" Fanny said. She glanced at him from beneath her thickly lashed eyelids. "How interesting." I knew Fanny would find that titillating. "Perhaps there're some things you can explain to me too," she went on. "Things I've always wanted to know. You look like you know an awful lot."

"Not very much about religion actually," Dick said.

"Oh, religion!" Fanny dismissed that subject with a shake of her head. "Things about college. You *are* a college man, aren't you?"

"Well, actually, not yet," Dick said. "But I know an awful lot about Rutgers. That's where my father went, and that's where I'm going to go. What do you want to know?"

I turned toward Peter. Obviously, I didn't have to worry about Dick any more than I had to worry about Mabel.

"Look, Peter," I said to him, "this service we're having here tonight—it's really a drama. It re-creates the

124 ·

exodus of the Jews from slavery in Egypt. That's really the beginning of the Jewish people." I opened the book that had been put beside his plate. "It's all in here," I said. "This little book—it's called the *Haggadah*—it tells the whole story." I opened the copy at my place too and showed it to him. "Mine's all in Hebrew," I said, "but yours has an English translation alongside the Hebrew so you can follow."

At the head of the table, Papa raised his glass and began to chant the *kiddush*. "Blessed art thou, O Lord our God, creator of the fruit of the vine. . . . Blessed art thou, O Lord our God, king of the universe, who hath sustained us in life, and enabled us to reach this joyous season." Everyone at the table, even little Maude, picked up his or her wine cup and drank—everyone except Peter.

"Go ahead, Peter," I said. "Drink some."

He looked at me and smiled sheepishly. "You know," he said, "I've never taken a drink before in front of grown-ups. Only with the fellows."

"Well then, it's time to start, old man." I smiled right into his eyes. "Here's looking at you," I said. "*L'chayim*—to life," and I drank down the whole glass. So did he.

"It's good," he said. "Sweet and good." The wine warmed him, and after that he relaxed.

My cousin Leo, the youngest child present able to memorize them, recited the four questions. "Why is this night different from all other nights? Why on this night do we eat only unleavened bread? Why on this night do we eat only bitter herbs and dip them twice?

· 125

On all other nights we eat either sitting up or reclining; why on this night do we all recline?"

Everything that followed was an answer to Leo's questions. "We were Pharaoh's slaves in Egypt, and the Lord our God brought us forth from there with a mighty hand and an outstretched arm." Henry translated everything for Mabel, even though she also had an English translation in her copy of the *Haggadah*. Dick and Fanny paid no attention whatsoever to what was going on, but whispered steadily about college, football, and who knows what else. Anyone looking at Peter's face and mine would have assumed our entire attention was directed at the service. We dutifully sipped our wine every time it was required of us. Under the table, however, Peter's fingers were drawing patterns first on the back and then on the palm of my hand. Every now and then, as if by accident, our knees would touch.

We came to the singing of "Daienu"—it would have been enough. It is a rousing tune no one can resist, and after the second repetition of the one-word chorus, Peter, Dick, and Mabel were singing it as loudly as the rest of us.

> *Dai—dai—enu*
> *Dai—dai—enu*
> *Dai—dai—enu*
> *Daienu, daienu!*

One by one, Papa held up the Passover symbols on the plate in front of him and explained their meaning. Softly I translated for Peter. "The burnt lamb bone—

that symbolizes the Passover sacrifice. When the lamb's blood was sprinkled on the doorposts of the Jews, the Angel of Death passed over those houses and killed the firstborn of only the Egyptians, so that Pharaoh would be persuaded at last to let the Jews go."

Papa held up the *matzoh*. "Unleavened bread," I whispered, "to remind us that we rushed out of Egypt so fast when Pharaoh finally let us go that our bread did not have time to rise." My whispering voice echoed Papa's sing-song Hebrew chanting. Peter's hand in mine, the wine, and the music made me feel as if I were drifting in some beautiful dream where for once everything had come together.

I made Peter taste the *charoses*—the delicious mixture of wine, honey, chopped apples, and nuts, which symbolized the mortar the Hebrew slaves had to make out of straw. The bitter horseradish dipped in salt water, which represented the toil and tragedy of slavery and death I could not persuade him to taste, but I ate it, and the bitterness on my tongue only emphasized the sweetness of the evening. When Papa held up the green parsley and the roasted egg, I whispered to Peter, "They're like the eggs and flowers in an Easter basket," I said. "They're for rebirth and spring and coming together." Peter squeezed my hand, and if I had died right then, I'd have died happy.

I had to get up to help Mama serve the meal. When I sat down again to eat, Peter smiled at me. "I didn't know it was going to be like this," he said. "I thought it was going to be serious—even gloomy. Why didn't you tell me?"

"I tried to," I replied, "but how could I? It's something you have to see for yourself."

"You love it, don't you?" he asked thoughtfully.

"Love what?"

"This," he said. His gesture included the whole table, everything on it, everyone at it, the very air surrounding it. "All of this."

"My family has done this for as long as I can remember," I said. "Jewish families all over the world are doing the very same thing at this very same minute, and they have done it for thousands and thousands of years, back almost to the beginning of recorded time." Peter nodded. Neither of us said anything for a moment, and then I giggled. "Though it's all a pain in the neck sometimes," I said. "You know."

"Yeah," he agreed.

"But I need it. I wouldn't feel whole without it." It felt good to talk to him again about things that mattered. In explaining things to him, I found that I was explaining them to myself.

Papa sent Ruthie to open the door for Elijah, the prophet of the Messiah, whose coming will mean an end to the sufferings and misery not only of the Jews but of all mankind. Elijah's cup of wine sat untouched in the middle of the table, as it did every year. But of course Elijah wasn't at the door when Ruthie opened it, any more than he had been any other year, or I guess ever will be. But it's funny how each time the door is opened, a person has this little knot of hope at the bottom of her stomach.

We had come to the singing of the long, many-versed hymns which make up the final part of the Seder service. It was late, but we had not yet reached the final song, "Chad Gad-Yo" ("One Only Kid"), a kind of theological "House That Jack Built" which was no doubt stuck at the very end to keep the children awake in anticipation of it. We were only on "Adir Hu" ("Who Knows One"), when there was a loud rap on the kitchen door—the only entrance from the outside into our apartment. It was startling to hear it. We were all suddenly silent, as if Elijah indeed had come. Who else, after all, could it be?

Ruthie scurried to open the door, but it was not Elijah who entered our kitchen. It was Mr. van Ruysdaal. Peter stood up, clutching his napkin tightly in his hand, the color suddenly drained from his face.

Papa rose too. "Won't you come in, Mr. van Ruysdaal?" he said graciously. "Perhaps you will join us in a glass of wine to mark the festivals of this season?"

"No, no, Mr. Levitsky," Mr. van Ruysdaal said hastily. "I can't do that." He looked around suspiciously, then suddenly recalled his manners. "Nice of you to ask," he said, "but we must go. It's getting kind of late. School tomorrow, you know. The boy said he was going out for dinner, and well, it got kind of late to just be having dinner. So the wife started to worry." He pulled his watch out of his vest pocket and glanced at it. "Close to midnight." Then he looked around the room. "Didn't realize you folks were having a party."

"It's sort of like Easter, Dad," Peter said. He had come through the parlor into the kitchen and was standing next to his father now. I had followed him.

It all seemed very strange to me. Peter was eighteen years old. I was sure his father was not in the habit of chasing after him every time he stayed out 'til midnight.

"Is it?" Mr. van Ruysdaal said. "That's very interesting. But let's go now. You too, Dick, Mabel," he called down to them. "I saw your father at the lodge meeting, Dick. He didn't know how I'd gotten the idea Peter was eating at your house. He said he expected you home by ten." Peter gave Dick a funny look, but he didn't say anything. I could imagine what my mother was thinking. "Humph. The *goyim* come chasing after their children to make sure we haven't murdered them to make *matzohs* out of their blood." But out loud she only said, "You're welcome," when Peter and the others thanked her for letting them come.

I got their coats for them from my bedroom and went out with them on the back porch. Mr. van Ruysdaal led the way. He was in a hurry and halfway down the stairs by the time Peter and Dick, who had insisted on saying goodnight to my parents and grandparents, shut the door behind them. I stood shivering in the cool spring night while Peter muttered to Dick, "Why did you tell your father where we were going? I told you to keep your mouth shut."

For once in his life, Dick stood up to Peter. "If my parents ask me a straight question, they get a straight answer," he said. "I don't lie to them. I don't have to." He clattered down the stairs without another word. Peter leaned over the railing and called down to his father, "Wait for me on the street. I'll be down in a second." He turned back to me. "I suppose you came out here for some kind of an explanation," he said. "I guess I owe you one."

"I don't know why I came out here," I said. "I don't think I need an explanation. You didn't tell your parents where you were going. You told them you were going to have supper at Dick's. But your father found out where you really were, and when it got late, he came over here to get you. He's very angry."

"I don't know how angry he really is, but my mother must be mad as hops," Peter said sadly. "She's sort of particular, you know. She gets upset when she doesn't know whose house I'm at."

She knew, I thought to myself, but she still got upset. I shook my head. "Peter," I said, "you talked so much about not sneaking around. But all this honesty, it was just supposed to go one way, is that it?"

"Becky, I didn't understand. Really and truly, I did not understand. I couldn't really believe that your mother objected to me. I could understand that *my* mother objected to you. But I couldn't really grasp that it worked the other way. I couldn't really see any reason for it, on your parents' part."

"Boy," I said, "that's really a pretty stuck-up thing to admit."

"Yeah, I know," he said. "I know that now. After tonight."

"Peter, come on," Mr. van Ruysdaal called from down below.

"Coming, Dad," he yelled. And then to me he said, "I guess I learned a lot tonight. I've got to go now." He put his hands on my shoulders and looked at me for a moment. The moon was full and the night was nearly as bright as day. "Good-bye, Becky. I just wanted you to know—I really did love you. I wasn't fooling." He didn't wait for me to reply. He turned and ran quickly and noisily down the wooden stairs.

"Goodnight," I called, my voice sounding strange and choked to my own ears.

"Good-bye," he said again from the bottom of the steps. Then he was gone.

I stood for a few moments on the porch, my hands clutching my arms. I was cold, but I didn't want to go in. I wasn't crying, though. There were tears in the back of my eyes, but that was where I made them stay. I was sober as a judge now, and perfectly able to control myself.

The back door opened and Ruthie stood outlined in the light from the kitchen. "Don't you want to come in?" she asked. "It's time to sing 'Chad Gad-Yo.' Mama said to tell you."

"All right," I replied. "I'm coming." She held the door for me, and I went in, taking my place again at the table.

"Too bad your friends had to leave," Henry said. "They're missing the best part."

"Oh, 'Chad Gad-Yo' stops being the best part after you're about ten," Fanny said. "I'm glad Dick left before we got to it. It's so silly." But she wasn't too sophisticated to sing along just as loud as the rest of us.

One only kid, one only kid, that my father bought
     for two *zuzim*. One only kid; one only kid.

> And came the cat and ate the kid that my father
> bought for two *zuzim*. One only kid; one only
> kid.
> And came the dog and bit the cat that ate the kid
> my father bought for two *zuzim*. One only kid,
> one only kid.
> And came the stick and beat the dog that bit the
> cat that ate the kid my father bought for two
> *zuzim*. One only kid; one only kid. . . .

I sang very loud too. I knew perfectly well that Mrs. van Ruysdaal would never have sent her husband after Peter if he had been at Dick's house or Mabel's house, instead of at the Jews' house. The golden dream in which I'd moved earlier in the evening was shattered like a broken mirror. Thank goodness for the song.

> And the Holy One, blessed be He, came and
> slaughtered the Angel of Death, who slaugh-
> tered the butcher, who butchered the ox, who
> drank the water, that put out the fire, that
> burned the stick, that beat the dog, that bit the
> cat, that ate the kid my father bought for two
> *zuzim*. One only kid; one only kid.

Like Peter, I had learned something this Seder night. I had learned that I was a Jew and I could never be anything else. I would never want to be anything else.

Shavuos

MAY CAME, and with it real sunshine, real spring at last. There were only six weeks left and then high school would be over for me forever. Still, what I was to do after graduation had not been settled. That is, it was settled so far as Mama and Papa were concerned. It was not settled so far as I was concerned.

I had written to Barnard for a catalog and application forms. They came on a Saturday when I was in the store and Matt, the postman, handed the mail to me. Thus, for better or worse, a confrontation was temporarily postponed. Papa gave me fifteen cents an hour when I helped in the store, so I had the five dollars I needed for the application fee. I bought a money order with it at the post office and sent it with the forms. I got the necessary "certificates of character" from Mr. Allison and Miss Krieter and our principal, Mr. Cranston. The school sent in a transcript of my grades too. It was a good transcript. I hadn't gotten anything other than an A as a final grade in any subject in three years of high school.

Toward the end of June, I'd have to go to New Brunswick and sit for the College Board exams. That would take four days at least. There was no way I could do that without Mama and Papa's knowing. But I wasn't worried about the exams themselves.

I knew Barnard would accept me. If they accepted Jews at all, and Sally Carruthers had assured me they did, they would accept me.

At night in the bathroom I pored over the catalog.

"Classical Literature 301. Greek Drama and Its Influences. The major Greek tragedies and comedies, and their influence on Roman and later European drama. Theories of comedy and tragedy including those of Aristotle. The production of plays. Professor Sheffield. MWF 11." "Greek 1-2. Elementary Full-Year Course. Grammar, composition, and reading. Professor Eaton. MWF 9-10." "Latin 301. Lyric Poetry. Selections from Catullus and Horace. Prerequisite: Latin 201 or four years of high school Latin. Professor Porter. TThSat 11-12." "History 412. Studies in the History of the Hellenistic World. Aspects of the history of the Hellenistic East: Interaction of Greeks and natives, administration, economy and society, royal politics. Professor Bagnall. MWF 2-3."

But what would happen when the letter acknowledging receipt of my credentials came? Matt would give Papa the mail in the store, and Papa would go through it right away as he always did. He would see the letter addressed to me—I never got any letters—and he would see the return address—"Barnard College, 3001 Broadway, New York, New York." What would happen then? I didn't know, but at least Papa would have to discuss my going to college, whether he wanted to or not.

I drank a lot of coffee and picked at Ruth constantly. However, at least Peter and I weren't enemies. It was not only that we understood each other better. We understood ourselves better. We did not go out of our way to meet, but when we did we spoke like old friends who had not seen each other for a long time, and had nothing in common except some memories of long ago. Our nipped-in-the-bud romance had begun for some right reasons, such as the fact that we really had had a great deal to say to each other and we had certainly enjoyed hugging and kissing. But it had begun for plenty of wrong reasons too, chief of which was a deeply felt desire to spit in our parents' eyes. It's strange how you can want to do that and love them so much all at the same time.

Early in June Annie came back. One day she just got off the train at Winter Hill and walked to the Klein house, carrying the same cardboard suitcase she had left with. She still had her key. She let herself in and when Sid came home from the store, he found her there, making blintzes, because it was Shavuos, and she asked if she might stay. He said yes, he would be glad to have her.

Sid told Papa she was back, and the next day I went to see her. It was the second day of Shavuos and she fed me some of her blintzes. A blintze is a thin pancake wrapped around cottage cheese or fruit, fried in butter, and served with sour cream. Annie's were superb. She had the light touch they required. While I gobbled them up, she told me about her return and apologized for not having written during her two-month absence. "I couldn't write," she said. "There was nothing to say. It was all too horrible."

"I'm glad you're back," I said as I wiped bits of sour cream and cottage cheese from my lips with the napkin she had given me. "I've missed you."

"I had to come back," she answered in a subdued

voice. She had only picked at the blintzes she had put on her own plate to keep me company, not even finishing one while I had eaten five. "I couldn't stay at my stepmother's house. I just couldn't. There was no room. Every day she found some other reason to complain about me, like my clothes. She couldn't stand the fact that I had nice clothes and they took up room in the closet. She thought I should pawn them and give her the money for board. We quarreled constantly. My poor father was being torn to bits. I tried to get a job so I could afford a room of my own someplace, but what can I do? Sew a little, that's all."

"Piece work?" I asked. "In a factory?"

"Exactly," she replied gloomily. "Piece work in a factory or scrubbing someone else's floor. You know me, Becky. I can't do those things. I just can't. I had no choice but to swallow my pride and come back. Maybe Sid will never understand me, nor I him. And maybe my mother-in-law will always hate me and I her. But I'd rather be their slave than the slave of the foreman in a shirt factory or of some rich old lady on Clinton Place!"

"Slave, Annie?" I repeated. "Slave? That's a pretty strong word!"

"But that's what I am," Annie insisted. "Even more so now. I shall have to do exactly what they say. Maybe someday Sid will love me again. If that happens, and we have a baby, things will be better. But I'll never be able to love him again. Never."

Hearing her talk like that hurt my heart. "Don't say that, Annie," I cried. "Don't say that. It can't be true."

But Annie only shook her head and smiled a small, sad smile. She was certainly not the same Annie who had stormed out of town right after Purim. The sparkle, the laughter, the flirtatious charm were all gone, at least for the time being. I could only hope that the girl Sid had fallen in love with would come back again, at least a little bit.

When I got home from Annie's, I found Henry Braude at our house. It was Friday, so that wasn't surprising. Mama had invited him for *shabbos* dinner again, I supposed, but he had come awfully early. Well, he'd done that once before too, sitting at the kitchen table, bothering us while we prepared the meal. I wished he'd go down to the store and talk to Papa. Perhaps he sensed that Papa didn't like him nearly as well as Mama. But no, that was impossible. He had not sensed that I didn't like him, so why should he imagine that Papa didn't? I was left with the unpleasant conclusion that he really wanted to be with me, or felt that he ought to be with me. I thought that for Henry the two were the same. With Henry, desire never seemed to interfere with duty. I could almost envy him that.

"Did you go to *minyan* this morning?" I asked him as I sat opposite him at the kitchen table, shelling peas.

"No," he said, "I have no time for the morning *minyan*. I have to open up the store."

"Papa goes every morning," I said.

"But you live in Winter Hill. It takes too long to come in from Brookville on the trolley."

"Henry can go with Papa tonight, before supper," Mama said.

"I'd like to go with Papa Levitsky," Henry said, "if he doesn't close the store too late."

Papa Levitsky? No one called my father Papa except Ruth and me. He wasn't old enough for that. He was barely forty. His hair and beard were still like my own hair—dark brown—shot through with glints of red, not gray.

However, when my father walked into the room a moment later, I noticed Henry was not about to take any liberties with him in person. "Good *shabbos*, Mr. Levitsky," he said. "Good *yontif*."

They shook hands, and then they went off to services in Allemand Hall while Mama and Ruth finished dinner. I went down into the store to help Gladys and Horace, Papa's clerks, take care of late customers and close up.

When they came back, we had dinner. Henry was much more subdued than usual. He seemed to have something on his mind. He sat next to me and was very attentive, constantly asking me if I wanted the salt or the applesauce or a piece of *challah*. But other than that, he was quiet, neglecting to provide us with his usual blow-by-blow account of everything that had taken place in Uncle Moishe's store during the week, coupled with his less-than-subtle indications of how much better he could have handled every crisis than Uncle Moishe did.

Luckily Ruth had plenty to say. Mama was too busy

serving us and eating to talk much, and I was pre-occupied with my own problems. All the boys who had applied to colleges had heard from them. A letter from Barnard still had not come. So Ruth, for once, held the stage unchallenged and she reveled in it. She didn't much care if no one listened, so long as no one interrupted.

After dinner, Henry suggested he and I go for a walk. I had known that was coming. I was much less willing to go walking with Henry now that I had no Peter from whom I needed to deflect attention.

"I have to help Mama clean up," I said.

"Oh, that's all right," Mama said. "There isn't much. Ruthie'll help me. You go ahead. It's such a beautiful evening. It'd be a crime to stay indoors."

I had no choice. I got my jacket and Henry and I went out.

We walked all the way down Main Street past stores and houses, until there was nothing on either side but farmers' fields. It wasn't Main Street anymore, but a country road called Van Zandt's Lane. When we came to Van Zandt's Brook, Henry suggested that we sit down on the big old fallen tree trunk that rested on the bank. It was a favorite spooning spot in Winter Hill, but it was deserted tonight. There was a fête at the high school field to raise money for the hospital. Everyone was there. I'd suggested to Henry that we go too, but he said he wanted to talk.

It was a clear, still night. I didn't mind sitting there with Henry, smelling the fresh, damp grass and listening to the night's soft noises. I didn't have to worry about Henry's trying anything.

But Henry surprised me. I shivered momentarily in a sudden little wind. It was still early June, after all, and the evening wasn't really warm. Suddenly I felt Henry's arm around me. I turned to look at him in amazement and he kissed me. He was no expert, but he was pretty obviously interested in learning.

I pushed him away. "Henry," I said, sounding like Elsie Dinsmore, "what does this mean?" I removed his arm from my shoulder.

"I'm sorry," Henry said. "I shouldn't have kissed you first, I should have told you first."

"Told me what first?" I asked.

"Your father and your mother gave me permission to ask you to marry me."

"Oh," I said shortly. I was more annoyed than surprised. "And are you?"

"Am I what?"

"Are you asking me to marry you?"

"Why, yes, Rebecca, of course I am." Now *he* sounded annoyed. Actually, I liked Henry better annoyed than romantic. "If I wasn't going to ask you to marry me, would I have kissed you?"

"I don't know, Henry," I replied. I was suddenly having great difficulty keeping from laughing. "It has happened. Men have kissed women they didn't mean to marry."

"But you're not that kind of girl," Henry replied, a faint note of horror in his voice.

"No? Maybe I am. Really, Henry, how much do you know about me?"

"Enough to know you're an awful tease," Henry said. "You're always making fun of me." There was no anger in his voice, only a touch of sadness. "I know—I know I'm somehow laughable, Rebecca. I don't know why. It's always been that way. Ever since I was a little boy. Perhaps it's because I do take life seriously." His voice was very quiet, all his strident pomposity gone. "But I think I'm a good man," he said, "and I know I'd make you a good husband."

Suddenly I felt very, very guilty for the way I had treated Henry. I had always, in my mind, accused him of being too blind to see anything but his own preconceptions of other people. Now, I realized, I had been the same, at least so far as he was concerned. And I had used him. All those months I had been seeing Peter, I had used him.

I reached out and took his hand. "Henry, I know you'd make a good husband. I know it. But do you think it would be wise to marry someone like me—someone who teases you? I think you should marry a girl who loves you. You don't deserve anything less than that."

"We'd come to love each other," Henry said. "Your mother and father did."

My parents' marriage had been arranged by their families only a few months after my mother had arrived in the United States. And they had come to love each other. But that didn't always happen. "What about your parents?" I asked.

Henry took a deep breath. "No," he said honestly. "I don't think they ever came to love each other. But look at all the people who pick their own husbands and wives because they think they love them, and then they find out they don't. That isn't any better than arranged marriages. Worse, I think."

"Ours would be an arranged marriage," I said. I tried to speak gently. I did not want to hurt Henry. But I felt I had to be firm. "Arranged by you and my parents. But I can't go along with that, Henry. This is the United States of America in the twentieth century and I can't go along with that."

"Your parents want me to marry you," Henry insisted. "They want it very much. I think your mother would have liked it if I'd spoken to you about it before this. I wanted them to speak about it to you first, though. But your father said that wouldn't do. He said you'd never marry me then."

I laughed a little. "Papa knows me very well," I said. "Look, Henry, I know they want you to marry me. But do you want to marry me? Really, do you?"

"I want to be married," Henry said. "It's time for me to be married. I'm very lonesome here."

"That's no answer, Henry," I said. "Do you want to marry *me*?"

Henry said nothing, for a moment. Then, in the bright moonlight, I could see him put his head in his hands and shake it slowly. "I don't know," he said, his voice muffled. "I don't know."

"Look, Henry," I said. "There's a long summer in front of us. We'll walk out. But walk out with some

other girls too. Like Ella Goldberg. Or Sadie Gratz."
Sadie was about five years older than Henry, but I was
reaching for any possibility. There weren't very many
single Jewish girls in Winter Hill, but I meant to try.
"I'll introduce you," I said. "Maybe I could have a
party," I went on, suddenly seized with inspiration. "I
could invite some people from New Brunswick. They
could come up on the trolley." Ella knew people in
New Brunswick. She'd tell me whom to invite.

"That would be nice," Henry said. His voice
sounded small and far away.

"Come, Henry, let's go home," I said. "We can talk
about it on the way." It was funny how in the moment
that I had refused to marry him, I liked Henry lots
better than I ever had. I pulled him up gently, and
then we started back.

"Your parents are going to be terribly disappointed,"
he said.

I agreed. "But they'll get over it," I said.

"Your mother's very worried about you." He
paused for a moment. "You and that *shegitz*," he
blurted.

For the first time that evening I really was shocked.
"She knew?" I cried. "She knew about Peter?"

Henry nodded. "She knew," he said.

"And she didn't do anything about it?"

"She would have, if it had gone on much longer,"
Henry told me. "She was afraid to confront you with
it. She was afraid you might do something very foolish
if she forbade you to see him."

So Mama knew me too. Mama knew me better than

144 •

I had ever dreamed. But of course she had known. After Passover, how could she not have known?

"Your Mama felt . . ." Henry hesitated for a moment. "Your Mama felt the time had come. You needed someone to love you, she said."

"Oh, I do Henry, I do," I agreed. "Everyone needs someone to love them. You and me both. But we can't settle for anything less than the real thing."

"If we knew what that was," Henry said.

How astute of him, I thought. Tonight I was seeing a Henry I hadn't known about. "Well," I said aloud, "we have to try to find out what the real thing is, don't we?" I really couldn't get over it, though. I couldn't get over the fact that my mother had never said one word to me about Peter, except for that first day with the umbrella.

Henry did not come upstairs with me. He went right to the corner to wait for the streetcar. We both agreed that it would be better if I explained things to Mama and Papa myself. Henry was embarrassed about seeing them. He seemed to feel that he had failed them somehow.

They were sitting at the kitchen table drinking tea. If they hadn't been expecting me to come home with a big announcement, they'd have gone to bed. If it had been any night but Friday, they'd have passed the time playing casino. As it was, Papa was reading his newspaper and Mama was just repeatedly stirring and sipping her hot, sweet glass of tea.

"Where's Henry?" Mama asked as soon as I walked through the door.

"Next time you tell Henry Braude he can marry me, I suggest you ask me first. I think I'd make that a general rule," I went on. "It applies to any candidate for my hand."

Papa put down his newspaper and gave me a long, hard look. I pretended not to notice, and hung my jacket on the hook on the back of the kitchen door. "How many other candidates do you think there'll be?" he asked at last.

"Do you think husbands grow on trees?" Mama added angrily.

"No," I said, trying to keep my anger out of my voice. "I don't think they do. But I don't care. I don't want a husband. Not now. Not Henry Braude. And maybe never. Maybe no one."

Mama tried to sound casual, but I could see her hand clenched into a fist. "Are you seeing Peter van Ruysdaal again?" she asked. "Is that why you turned down Henry Braude?"

"Oh, Mama," I cried, "this has nothing to do with Peter. I don't want to marry Henry, but I certainly don't want to marry Peter. I swear to you, I'll never marry anyone who isn't Jewish, I swear it." I ran to her and knelt beside her, putting my arms around her. "I'm so sorry, Mama, I'm so sorry. But don't make me marry Henry Braude. Don't make me marry Henry Braude because of Peter!"

"Don't be silly, Rifka," Mama said. "No one is going to make you marry anyone you don't want to marry. I don't think we could if we would," she added with a sigh.

I stood up smiling a little. "No, I guess not," I said. I sat down in the chair between them.

"I told you, Molly," Papa said. "I told you it had nothing to do with Peter. Not after what happened at Passover."

"It's not only that . . ." I began.

Papa held up his hand and I fell silent. "You turned Henry Braude down because of this, didn't you?" he asked. From his inside vest pocket he pulled out an envelope and put it down in front of me. It was addressed to me, and it was from Barnard. I turned it over. It had been opened.

"Papa," I cried. "It isn't bad enough you tell people they can marry me. You open my mail too! When did this come?"

"It came today," Papa said. "And I didn't tell Henry he could marry you. I told him he could marry you if he had your consent. He said he didn't think that would be any problem."

"He said," Mama added, "that you had given him—well, indications, certain indications that you were fond of him."

Oh, that kiss. That fateful kiss way back in January. I told myself to remember that if I were ever going to kiss anyone experimentally again, I'd better make sure he regarded kissing in the same light I did.

"Frankly," Papa went on, "I told him I could hardly believe it. In my presence you had certainly never acted very fond of him. But he informed me that he knew all about that. Girls acted different in private. As a husband of twenty years and the father of two daughters, I was most grateful for his lessons in feminine psychology. He seemed so sure of himself." Papa shook his head and gave me a small smile. It seemed to me he wasn't really very sorry I would not marry Henry Braude.

"Papa," I said, "I wouldn't have married Henry Braude under any circumstances. Not willingly anyway. Barnard has nothing to do with it. Do you understand that?"

Papa nodded. "I believe you," he said.

"What does my letter from Barnard say?" I asked.

"Why don't you read it and find out?"

"I'm afraid to," I admitted. Suddenly my certainty that I would be accepted had vanished. No doubt, it suddenly occurred to me, all the applicants to Barnard had as good a record as I did. Otherwise, why would they apply? But Papa was looking at me. I pulled the letter out of the envelope and unfolded it slowly.

My dear Miss Levitsky:

The Committee on Admissions was most favorably impressed with your fine record, and it gives me great pleasure to write that you will be admitted to Barnard College as a student for the academic year commencing in September. This decision is subject to the satisfactory completion of your year's work in secondary school, and a satisfactory performance on the College Board Entrance Examinations, for which you have indicated you prefer to sit rather than for Columbia University's entrance examinations. A health report acceptable to the college physician will also be required.

In addition, I would like to inform you that your record and the most enthusiastic recommendations of your high school instructors make it worth your while to apply for one of Barnard's competitive scholarships for entering freshmen. Please fill out the enclosed forms and return them to me, making sure as well to inform the College Entrance Examination Board for which scholarship you wish to be considered.

We anticipate satisfactory completion of your entrance requirements and look forward to welcoming you in September as a member of the class of 1921.

With all good wishes, I am most sincerely yours,
Katherine S. Doty, A.M.
Secretary of the College.

I would have been excited if I had known I could go. But I did not know that. And so instead of a warm glow of pleasure, the familiar nausea rose into my throat. "Please," I said. "Please, Papa, can I go?"

"You can't go," Mama said. "How can you go? What will you eat?"

"Mama," I said, trying to be as calm ·as I could, "I've thought about that. I'll live with Bubbie and Zadie. I'll go up to Barnard every day on the subway. I'll carry my lunch in a paper sack. You know Bubbie and Zadie will be glad to have me come. They're lonesome in that apartment all by themselves, now that even Uncle Max is gone. Please, Mama. I promise you that in four years not one morsel of *treife* food will ever pass my lips. May I fall down dead on the spot if it does!"

"Don't make any promises you're not going to keep," Papa said dryly. "Four years is a long time."

I turned to him, hardly daring to believe my ears. "I can go? Do you mean it, Papa, I can really go?"

"Tell them to keep their scholarship," Papa said. "No daughter of mine has to go to college on charity. We'll use the money we put away for your wedding."

"But, Chaim," Mama objected, "someday she will get married. Surely she'll get married someday!"

"By then there'll be more, Molly," Papa said. "How many times have I told you? About money we don't have to worry."

"Papa," I asked softly, "Papa, please tell me. What made you change your mind?"

"I did what you told me to do, Rifkele," he replied gently. "I thought about Annie. No daughter of mine is going to end up like that," he said. "Especially a daughter that a college gives scholarships to, without her even asking. I don't want any lives wasted around here."

"Thank you, Papa," I said, giving him a big hug and kiss. "And you, Mama," I said, turning to her. "What made you change your mind?"

"Me change my mind?" Mama said. "Humph! I haven't changed my mind. Believe me, I don't like where this is going to end."

"Mama, where *is* it going to end?"

"I don't know, but I don't like it." She shook her head glumly. "But between you and your father, how can I argue? Go," she shrugged. "Go in good health. Just remember one thing. Remember who you are."

"I'll remember, Mama," I promised. If I know, I thought. But it seemed I was finding out. Beginning to, anyway.

Rosh Hashanah

As it turned out, I was the valedictorian of the class. I delivered a speech on the Elizabethan theater in honor of the tercentenary of Shakespeare's death. The whole graduation was around a Shakesperian theme. Peter delivered Antony's funeral oration from *Julius Caesar* and Mabel and Gilbert Smith did a scene from *As You Like It*. The whole class sang "O Mistress Mine" and "Where the Bee Sucks There Suck I," both a little risqué for a high school graduation, but no one noticed that because they were by Shakespeare. It was a nice graduation. I liked it a lot better than the baccalaureate service at the Dutch Reformed Church, during which the Reverend Mr. Baumann urged us to lead pure Christian lives.

In between getting ready for graduation I studied for the College Board Entrance Examinations. I sat for examinations in math, history, German, botany, Latin, French, and English. I made a mess of the botany, performed passably in math and history and excelled in the languages. No surprises.

After the exams, I spent my spare time reading. When I was feeling energetic, I read Horace and Catullus and the Bible in Hebrew, so I'd be better prepared for Barnard. When I was feeling lazy, I read Booth Tarkington's latest, *Seventeen*. It was amusing, but it wasn't about me.

I didn't have very much time for reading anyway. I spent a large part of each day in the store. My being there freed Papa to spend hours checking progress on the construction of the new *shul*. All summer long we watched it go up on the corner of Stryker and East Main streets, piece by piece, until its yellow stucco walls and stained glass windows in memory of Mr. Baumgartner's father and Mr. Polansky's mother and my own unknown Levitsky grandparents were all in place. Mr. Polansky and Mr. Baumgartner, as well as my father, were there every day along with Mr. Gordon, the sexton, nagging the painters and carpenters so that every last pew would be in place in time for the high holy days, Rosh Hashanah and Yom Kippur.

Rosh Hashanah means "head of the year." It is the birthday of the world, the anniversary of creation, when all Jews gather in the synagogue to praise the glory of God. It ushers in a whole week of prayer and repentance, which is climaxed by Yom Kippur, the Day of Atonement. Like all other peoples, Jews want to begin the New Year with a clean slate, free of the sins of the past.

This year, Rosh Hashanah was special. The evening the holiday began, we marched the *torah* from Allemand Hall to our new synagogue, B'nai Avraham.

"Remember today," Papa said as we stood out in front of the store waiting while he locked the door. We were all dressed in our very best. I was wearing a brand new suit Mama had bought me for going away to school. With my hair swept up and a big ostrich plume on my dashing wide-brimmed hat, I felt sophisticated enough to take on the whole of New York City single-handed. Ruth had on a beautiful white eyelet dress with a pale blue sash that Mama had made for her. Even Mama had discarded the black dress she always wore for going to *shul* and had treated herself to a sand-colored suit with a seven-gored skirt and a dark-red velvet collar. I guess Mama had at last come to believe Papa when he said we had enough money. Papa always dressed well, and today he had on a perfectly cut dark-gray suit, a black bowler hat, black shoes with white spats and pearl-gray gloves. He carried an ebony walking stick with a gold handle.

"Remember today," Papa said. "It's not likely you'll see another *torah* parade in your lifetime. It isn't the kind of thing that happens every day."

"I hope you don't have to remember being pelted with rotten tomatoes, or rocks, or worse," Mama said. "The way Rifka was the day I sent her for the chicken."

"What I love about you, Mama," I said, "is your eternal optimism. It's wonderful how you always look on the bright side of things."

"Rebecca, don't talk fresh to your mother," Papa said automatically.

I was walking next to my mother, and I put my arm around her and gave her a hug. "I'm so happy, Mama," I said. "You be happy too." Monday I would be at Barnard for the start of the fall term. I would have to celebrate Yom Kippur with Bubbie and Zadie in New York. I could not imagine a holiday without my parents and Ruthie.

When we got to Allemand Hall, Papa went inside with the other men who had gathered there. We women waited outside in the golden light of late afternoon. It was September, and though the day was warm as summer there was that hint of autumn in the air, that precious quality to the sunshine that makes your heart ache for the summer that slipped so quickly through your fingers. That day my heart ached too for my family and for my childhood and for all of Winter Hill. Already I was a little bit homesick. I was learning that for everything you get in this life, you make some kind of payment.

The men came out, carrying the *torahs*. The women separated and made a kind of aisle for them to pass through. Mother and I and some of the others put our fingers to our lips and then touched those fingers to the holy scrolls as they passed by. O'Hagan, the cop, went first, on his horse, to clear the road for us. Next came the rabbi and then all the other men and boys in the congregation. The women and girls brought up the rear.

We started down Main Street quietly. As they walked, the men passed the *torah* scrolls from one to the other, so every male in the congregation would have the honor of carrying one for a bit of the way.

At first there was no sound except the shuffle of our feet as we walked down the middle of the street, and the soft murmur of our conversation. Allemand Hall was on Carver Street, near the lace works. An occasional homeward-bound worker stared at us as we walked by but the street was largely deserted.

When we got to Main Street proper, things were different. It was still early so many people were on the street, and they paused to stare at us. "Look, Mama," a little boy cried. "The Jews are coming!"

"See?" Mama said to me. "What did I tell you. The next thing you know, he'll throw tomatoes."

But the boy's voice had not sounded hostile to me. Only curious. I looked at the faces of the people along the sidewalk. I saw no hostility in them either—only that same curiosity.

I turned to Ruthie. "Let's sing," I whispered.

She shook her head. "I'm afraid."

"If we start," I said, "everyone else will join in. Come on, let's try." We both had good strong voices and we knew all the songs. I began, as loud as I could,

> *Hevenu shalom aleichem*
> *Hevenu shalom aleichem*

Ruthie joined in, hesitantly at first, but louder as we moved along.

> *Hevenu shalom aleichem*
> *Hevenu shalom, shalom, shalom aleichem.*

All around us, the voices of the other women picked up the tune. And then the men began to join in too. Soon we were all singing, all one hundred and fifty of us as we walked down Main Street.

> *Hevenu shalom aleichem*
> *Hevenu shalom aleichem*
> *Hevenu shalom aleichem*
> *Hevenu shalom, shalom, shalom aleichem.*

We were all smiling too, suddenly seized by a feeling

156 ·

of great joy. Even Mama was smiling and singing. The *torah* scrolls were lifted high in front of us, and we marched behind strong in the company of each other, chanting loudly for the glory of God and the Jewish faith.

More and more people were coming out of the stores, lining the street to watch us go by. I saw Mabel, leaving her job at Woolworth's with Dick Evans at her side. That was a new thing. They saw me, and waved. I waved back. Other people waved at those of us in the parade whom they knew, and we returned their greetings. We were all smiling, marchers and watchers. And we marchers never stopped singing.

> *V'taheyr libeynu*
> *V'taheyr libeynu*
> *V'taheyr libeynu*
> *L'ovd'cho be-e'mes.*

There was Peter, standing in front of the hardware store with his father. I smiled and waved at him as soon as I saw him. I had not seen him all summer. He smiled and waved back at me, hard as he could, and even his father tipped his hat as we passed him by.

> *La la la*
> *Lala Lala La*
> *L'ovd'cho be-e'mes.*

Henry Braude was in the rear line of the marching men and Ella Goldberg was in the front line of marching women. All of a sudden I noticed that they were walking side by side, Ella's arm linked through

Henry's. The party with the young people from New Brunswick that I had promised Henry had never taken place. Once she met him, Ella was not interested in introducing Henry to anyone else, and Henry seemed well-satisfied with the arrangement.

Sid Klein hung back for a moment, and when Annie caught up with him, he took her arm and they went on together. Soon all the men and all the women were mixed up. We were no longer marching by sex; we were marching by family. And still we were singing, as loud as we could, carried along in a cloud of elation.

Shalom aleichem mala'chey ha sho reys
Mala'chey el yon.

We reached the synagogue at last. The men who had taken the lead in its building took the *torah* scrolls from those who had carried them to the door. The rest of us went on inside while they stayed behind, waiting for us to take our seats in the shiny new pews of golden oak. The men sat downstairs, surrounding the heavy new mahogany reading desk. We women climbed up-stairs to our seats in the balcony—still separate, but no longer behind a screen. Now at least the women in the front rows might possibly have the feeling that they were actually present at a service.

When we were all seated the men came in carrying the scrolls. Papa was one of them. How proud we were, Mama and Ruthie and I, that he was among the half dozen to be so honored. We all stood up again as the scrolls of the law were marched down the aisle and placed, gently, reverently, in the open ark against the eastern wall. Again, we were all singing.

Kee lekach tov nahsatee lachem
Torahsee al ta-ahzovu.
Etz chayim hee lamachzikim bah v'somchehah me-ushar.
Deracheha darchay no-am v'chol-neseevoseha shalom.
Hasheevenu Adonoy elecha v'noshuvah
Chadesh yamaynu k'kedem.

I looked around me at all my friends and neighbors, singing together. In three days I would be gone. For the moment, though, just for that moment, the song and its singers surrounded the six scrolls in their purple velvet, gold-embroidered wrappers, as they rested in the satin-lined ark. The song surrounded me too.

> I have given you good teaching;
> Forsake not My Torah.
> It is a tree of life to them that hold fast to it,
> And everyone that upholds it is happy.
> Its ways are ways of pleasantness,
> And all its paths are peace.
> Turn us unto Thee, O Lord, and we shall return;
> Renew our days as of old.

That is what the song we sang meant. And though a thousand years have passed since then, still I remember it as if it happened yesterday.

About the Author

Barbara Cohen is the author of THE CARP IN THE BATH-TUB, THANK YOU, JACKIE ROBINSON and WHERE'S FLOR-RIE? A high school English teacher and a newspaper columnist, she lives in a small town in New Jersey with her husband Eugene and their three daughters, Leah, Sara and Rebecca.